A Man
With a Pure Heart

by

Linda Tillis

A sequel to A Heart Made for Love

A Man With a Pure Heart

Cover Art by *Debbie Taylor*

The Wild Rose Press, Inc.
PO Box 708
Adams Basin, NY 14410-0708
Visit us at www.thewildrosepress.com

Publishing History
First Vintage Rose Edition, 2017
Print ISBN 978-1-5092-1360-3
Digital ISBN 978-1-5092-1361-0

A sequel to A Heart Made for Love
Published in the United States of America

"Tell me where to look and I'll find the animal who did this. Give me somewhere to start, and then you can be at peace with the angels," the man whispered softly, as he gently uncovered her face. The photographer didn't flinch, but the younger man was unable to hold in a shocked gasp. The only recognizable part of the woman's face was at the corner of her left eye, where two moles were evident against white skin. The face had been punched, and punched again and again.

Samuel Hinton rose to his full six foot five inches and looked slowly around the room. His eyes took in the four walls of the old abandoned cabin. The broken chair and three-legged table were covered in what was, probably, years of dust. Vines had welcomed themselves in through windows long ago broken, and some had even entered through the rotten floor.

Only the dust in the corner where the woman lay had been disturbed. Samuel was careful not to step on the already present prints. The killer would be a large man. The foot that made those marks would be about the size of his. But it wasn't really a boot…or a shoe, he thought. He could plainly see the outline of his own boot. The killer's was more of a scuff, or a…moccasin! Ah, a moccasin. He looked at the bruises on the woman's upper arms. They were larger than even his hands would have made. Yep, he was a big one.

Dedication

To the men and women of Law Enforcement,
who deal with death and mayhem every day,
I salute your perseverance, your dedication to duty,
and the courage which causes you
to put your life on the line for me and mine.
Thank you.

~

And of course, to my Beau,
who keeps me centered with his unwavering support.

Chapter One

There were three men in the room. That is, three men and a dead woman. They were deep in the woods, southwest of Tallahassee.

Two of the men stood stiffly in the corner, just inside the open doorway. The door itself hung askew, held only by the rusted lower hinge. These two had been cautioned by their commanding officer not to move, speak, or otherwise disturb the third man. One was there to photograph at the direction of the tall man, and the youngest of the three had been told to be quiet and learn.

The third, a very tall man, knelt by the woman. She was small in stature, and completely naked. Long, thick hanks of copper-colored hair covered her face.

The two in the corner turned questioningly to each other. Was he actually speaking to the woman? It was just a whisper and neither of the two could make out his words.

"Tell me where to look and I'll find the animal who did this. Give me somewhere to start, and then you can be at peace with the angels," the man whispered softly, as he gently uncovered her face. The photographer didn't flinch, but the younger man was unable to hold in a shocked gasp. The only recognizable part of the woman's face was at the corner of her left eye, where two moles were evident against white skin.

The face had been punched, and punched again and again.

Samuel Hinton rose to his full six foot five inches and looked slowly around the room. His eyes took in the four walls of the old abandoned cabin. The broken chair and three-legged table were covered in what was, probably, years of dust. Vines had welcomed themselves in through windows long ago broken, and some had even entered through the rotten floor.

Only the dust in the corner where the woman lay had been disturbed. Samuel was careful not to step on the already present prints. The killer would be a large man. The foot that made those marks would be about the size of his. But it wasn't really a boot...or a shoe, he thought. He could plainly see the outline of his own boot. The killer's was more of a scuff, or a...moccasin! Ah, a moccasin. He looked at the bruises on the woman's upper arms. They were larger than even his hands would have made. Yep, he was a big one.

Samuel stood and spoke to the photographer. "Be sure to get the bruises on her arms."

Samuel leaned against the doorframe and stared out through the trees, as the photographer set up his equipment. He could hear the tap-tap-tap of a woodpecker somewhere close by. Samuel suddenly pushed off and crossed the clearing. He stopped near the edge of the forest and knelt slowly. The youngest man stared from the doorway as Samuel reached into his pocket and pulled out a handkerchief-sized square of linen. He picked up something from the ground and held it close to his face. Then he placed it in the linen and carefully put it in his pocket. He walked back inside and knelt by the woman; with the thumb of his right hand, he gently raised her upper lip. He lowered the lip, raised her right hand, and looked at the long fingers for a while.

The younger man cleared his throat, and the photographer shot him a warning look. Samuel turned to him. "Yes, you have a question?"

"Y-yes, sir," he stuttered. "Why did you look in her mouth?"

"Well," Samuel drawled, "I found a cigarette butt on the ground. It looks like somebody's been smoking. Her teeth are very white, and her hands have no tobacco stains. If she smoked that cigarette, then it was probably the first one she ever smoked." As Samuel stood and turned to the door, the young man spoke again.

"But why did you take the cigarette, sir?"

Samuel let out a long sigh. It wasn't like he minded the questions. He didn't. He just didn't feel qualified to be training these boys. Shoot fire, he'd only graduated from the Academy in 1908 himself. He believed Captain Lance should have named an older, more experienced man to train these green ones. Two years on the job did not make him an expert. Besides, what Samuel had to share could not be spoken of, or written in a manual. There was no way he could tell them about the feelings that washed over him, or the visits from his mama, who had died when he was eight. No one outside his family would understand.

He turned to the young man again. "If the cigarette is not hers, then it probably belongs to the killer. The tobacco has an unusual aroma and might help us locate the man."

Samuel could tell when the young man made the mental connection. His eyes widened in surprise, then focused on Samuel in awe. Now that, Samuel did mind. Most of what he did was common sense; paying attention to detail and just looking at things with open eyes. He was no one special. He was just a man whose heart hated violence, especially violence to women.

****

Samuel Hinton sat on a bale of hay, staring across the meadow. The sun had dropped below the horizon and the sky was streaked with orange and pinks. He held a chunk of wood in each hand, weighing one against the other. He waited for one of them to speak to him. He would listen; then whatever was locked inside the wood would call to him, and he would carve something beautiful, releasing the spirit hidden in the wood. It had been this way since he was a child. Things just spoke to him. Sometimes people spoke to him, and sometimes the people were dead.

The woman he'd knelt by this morning had told him some things. It had been early morning, well before dawn, and she had been walking to the schoolhouse. A man with large hands had grabbed her. But where, where did this happen? She had smelled a strong yeastiness in the air. Had she been near a bakery?

He would give this more attention in the days to come, but now it was suppertime, and afterwards he would have a few minutes to play with his beautiful niece before Mae put her to bed.

****

Samuel woke from a deep sleep with all his senses immediately alert. He sensed the whisper of a voice, and it soothed him. He didn't need his eyes to tell him Mama was in the room, but the strong smell of yeast caused him to bolt upright. She was seated on the bench near the large window. He sensed that when he spoke she would begin to slip away, so he just sat there, absorbing her presence.

Then her melodious voice spoke. "You must hurry, Samuel. Another is in danger."

Even as he asked, she began to fade. "Who, Mama, who is in danger?" But she was already gone.

Samuel checked the clock as he slipped out of his apartment over the garage. Three in the morning, and here he was starting his day. Mae would not approve. He pushed his motorcycle a good quarter mile down the lane before heading into town for an early walk.

He had never spoken of Mama's visits when he was a child. Even though he had never been frightened by her presence, he hadn't been sure how others would react. Then the day had come when his sister had been in grave danger. Mama had appeared to him in front of others, but they hadn't seen or heard her. Later, he'd tried to explain it to his Pa, who had assured him he was not crazy.

Samuel laughed to himself as he strolled through the pre-dawn hours. He could laugh now, but that night, when Mae had been in danger of slipping away from them, poor Edward had met Mama. You could say it was a "come to Jesus" meeting. But all had gone well, Mae had recovered, and she and Edward had been married these past five years.

Samuel suddenly stopped walking. He was in one of the narrow service alleys behind the Leon Hotel. There was a slight breeze coming out of the southwest, and on the breeze was the distinct aroma of yeast. He started moving in a southwesterly direction, tacking up and down the empty streets, pausing occasionally to make sure he had not lost the smell he followed. He was moving away from the hotels and boarding houses when suddenly it hit him. The brewery. Damnation, he should have made the yeast connection.

He picked up his pace, being careful to stay in the shadows and walk softly.

Hamish McDuff had a small alehouse about three blocks south, and Samuel was headed there when the now familiar feeling washed over him. He paused to lean against the side of a building and fight the nausea. He straightened up and took deep breaths, then tried to pierce the darkness with keen eyes. He never anticipated what he was looking for, but he always found something. He walked out into the intersection. The city had built the road on each side of a towering live oak whose canopy created a huge circle of blackness on this moonless night. Samuel walked to the base of the tree and knelt. He closed his eyes and let his other senses take over.

After a few moments, his mind began to translate. In the far distance, he heard the faint crow of a rooster. Much closer came the almost silent whoosh of an owl's wings and the tiny squeak of a mouse. Then, from very near, an odd aroma. Oh, not the smell of McDuff's yeasty beer brewing. No, this was the curious fragrance of the cigarette butts he'd found by the cabin. Samuel opened his eyes and looked at the ground around him. Barely visible in the darkness were two cigarette butts. Samuel took another square of linen from his pocket and secured both in the square, then passed them under his nose. He actually smiled in the darkness. Now he knew where.

Chapter Two

Samuel was headed to Captain Lance's office for a status meeting when he heard the woman. She had a lovely voice, but right now it was raised in anger. He turned down the hallway to the office, and there she was, standing in front of Edith Hampton's desk. She was a sight to behold. She was at least six feet tall, wearing a dark blue traveling suit with a small matching, but useless, hat. No hat would ever be able to tame that hair. He had never seen such riotous, curly hair, and it could only be described as flaming.

Edith turned to him in relief. "Miss, this is the detective who is handling your sister's case. He will be able to answer all your questions." Edith raised pleading eyes to Samuel. He considered trying to duck into the captain's office, but he was too late.

The statuesque redhead turned and pinned him with the greenest eyes he'd ever seen.

"Well, sir, your name, please?" Samuel had been right. When her voice was not raised in anger, it was low in tone, and musical.

"My name is Samuel Hinton, miss, and you are?"

She extended her hand. "I am Kathleen Campbell. I have traveled from Boston to find out what happened to my sister…" Her voice faltered as she swayed, and those beautiful eyes became pools that dripped tears down her porcelain cheeks.

7

Samuel immediately pictured the late Mary Elizabeth Campbell in his mind, with her battered face covered by the swath of red hair.

The woman's tears tore at his heart. "Miss Campbell, please have a seat here." He directed her to a chair. "Edith, can you get Miss Campbell a glass of water, or maybe some tea?"

"I'm sorry, I've been traveling for two days. I don't remember when I last ate or slept." She looked up at Samuel, and he could see her inner pain reflected in her eyes.

"Miss…"

She interrupted him. "Please, call me Kathleen."

"All right, Kathleen. We have time to discuss your sister. Right now, I think maybe you need some food." As Edith returned with a glass of water, Samuel said, "Edith, tell Captain Lance I'll be back in an hour."

He could almost feel the look he suspected Edith was giving his back as he helped Kathleen Campbell to stand. One of these days, they were going to have to talk.

Twenty minutes later, he had Miss Campbell seated in a small diner a few blocks away. Samuel told the waitress, "Some orange juice, scrambled eggs, and buttered grits, for two, please."

Kathleen started to protest, but he cut her off. "I insist, Miss Campbell. My brother-in-law is a doctor, and he swears you have to have a good breakfast if you're gonna make it through the day."

Kathleen gave a weak smile. "You're too kind. I'm sorry to be so…so…darn girlish. Mary Elizabeth was half my size, but she was twice as strong."

Samuel smiled at this. It was the first time he'd

ever known a woman to apologize for being a woman, especially one as beautiful as this one.

"Kathleen, sometimes it's enough to just be who we are."

She took a long look at the man across the table. She'd been so upset earlier that she hadn't paid much attention to him, other than to notice how tall he was. He was ruggedly handsome, with a chiseled jawline, dark wavy hair, and eyes so light a brown as to appear gold. His slow, southern drawl made her hang on his every word.

The waitress arrived with their food, and Kathleen realized she'd been staring into Samuel's eyes for a good long minute.

They ate in silence. Kathleen finally swallowed the last of her juice, wiped her mouth, and then folded the napkin on the table.

"Thank you. You were right. I was in need of strength, and breakfast was delicious."

Samuel leaned back in his chair and nodded his acceptance of her thanks.

Her look turned somber again. "Now, sir, can you tell me what happened to my sister?"

"Tell me what you already know, and I'll try to fill in the gaps," he answered. He needed to know what she'd been told before he started to blurt out things that might hurt her.

"One of the local police officers came to our home with a telegram. He told us Mary Elizabeth had been reported missing and the resulting search had located her body. They advised foul play was suspected. My father is in Ireland on business, and my poor mother has taken to her bed. I made all the necessary arrangements." Kathleen clasped her hands together on the table to stop their trembling.

Samuel reached out and took her hands in his. She seemed to take strength from his touch and continued, "We held a small service and then laid Mary to rest. Father will be home in a few weeks, but Mother could not bear the wait…so here I am." She raised her face to him expectantly.

Samuel hated telling her the things she wanted to know. It was the part of his job he took to heart. "Your sister was teaching primary classes at a small school, on the western edge of town. As best we can tell, she would leave her small cottage in the early morning hours and walk to school. When the children arrived that morning, the school was still locked up. After an hour or so, one of the older ones walked home and told his mother the teacher had not shown up. She walked the mile or so to where Mary lived, but she couldn't find her. That's when we were contacted."

Kathleen nodded, "Mary Elizabeth was always an early riser. She had trouble sleeping, and it was not unusual for her to start her day at three or four in the morning. Please, go on."

Samuel became aware he still held her hands. He laid them flat on the table, and placed his on top. "It was past noon by the time the search began. We…I found Mary the next day in an old abandoned cabin, a couple of miles into the woods near the river. She had been killed by someone."

Halfway through his explanation, Kathleen closed her eyes, as if it would be less painful if she did not see him speak the words. Now she straightened in the chair. Her eyes opened, and Samuel was shocked by her expression. In truth, her lovely green eyes had darkened, and while they were full of tears, they were also full of hate.

"Have you found him? Do you have the man who killed my sister?"

Samuel understood her anger. This was her family they were talking about. Her sister. She had been unable to prevent this horrible act, and now she was going to make sure justice was delivered. Yes, Samuel understood. He had been willing, at the age of fifteen, to kill the men who had attacked his sister, Mae.

"No, I don't have him, yet. But I will."

Now Kathleen grabbed both of Samuel's hands. "Swear to me," she demanded. "Swear to me you will find this animal."

He looked straight into those dark green eyes and said, "This man will be found. And he will be held accountable for his actions. I promise you this."

Kathleen believed him. He seemed to understand her need for closure. She stood now. "Well, I've come to finish out the school year for my sister. It's what she would have wanted. So I will be here when you find him."

She was not leaving. She was going to be here, in Tallahassee, for several months. Now why should that make Samuel feel so darn good?

Samuel dropped Kathleen at her sister's cottage. "Kathleen, I will keep in touch. If I can help with anything, please let me know."

"You've already helped. I will begin work at the school on Monday morning. If you have information for me, I will be here or at the school. Thank you again for breakfast."

****

Edith Hampton had no smile for him on his return. "Well, did you get her all sorted out?"

"Yes, Edith, I did. Is the captain in?"

"Yes, and he's waiting for you."

Samuel had never given her reason to consider him anything other than a friend, but over the last few months she had taken on an air of ownership. It hadn't bothered Samuel until this morning, and that in itself was odd.

He knocked on the doorframe. Captain Lance looked up and motioned him in.

"Good morning, sir."

"Good morning to you, Detective. You have information for me? Edith said you were on your way to see me when a giant redhead kidnapped you," he said with a grin.

Samuel exhaled slowly, shook his head, and drawled, "Well, there was a redhead involved. She is Kathleen Campbell, the sister of our schoolteacher. But that can wait. I know where our killer picked up Mary Elizabeth."

The grin was gone in a flash. "Let's have it, then."

"On a hunch, I walked a route from the young lady's cottage to the school." He said nothing of the smell of yeast. "You know the huge live oak at the corner of Holmes and Maple? Well, I found these at the base of the tree." Samuel pulled the second linen square from his pocket and opened it up.

The captain looked at the contents, then back at Samuel. "Same as the ones near the cabin?"

"Yep, same odd aroma. I'm takin' these to a tobacconist later, to see what I can find out."

"Good. Just keep me posted. The paper ran another article this morning about how we have failed to find the killer. Not that I care much one way or the other what they say, but I don't like the idea of him running free, out there somewhere."

Samuel looked at the sky as he left the building. It was overcast, and a cool breeze ruffled his dark hair. It was the first week of October, and already there were good indications of fall leading into a cold winter. The leaves didn't turn red and yellow, like they did in North Georgia, but they did fall, and some trees were beginning to look a little thin.

He mentally marked items off a to-do list. The patrol sergeant would have four deputies all over the area surrounding McDuff's brewery. They would be questioning any residents thoroughly. Folks loved to talk; if the information was out there, someone would give it up.

Samuel let Kathleen Campbell run through his mind as he walked. She was beautiful, intelligent, and fiercely protective of her family; all admirable qualities to be found in a woman. He wondered what her laughter sounded like; maybe it would be like the water in a cold stream, rippling over rocks. Samuel missed a step and then shook his head at his own foolishness.

He'd barely met the woman, and here he was daydreaming about her laughter. Right now the poor woman had nothing to laugh about. It was clear to see she was devastated by her sister's death. Samuel wished he had more to tell her, but they were having a hard time developing a suspect.

He was sure that in time something would come to him. He was also sure the information would come without warning, and without any effort on his part. There was no need for him to agonize over it or beat himself over the head. He had no control over the situation. It came when it came.

Samuel opened the door to the tobacco shop and stopped abruptly. His senses were assailed by at least a dozen different aromas. The interior of the shop was not large, and the air was thick with the aroma of so many different blends of tobacco. The bell over the door had summoned a small, old gentleman from the back of the shop. He was all of five feet tall, slim, and had a full head of white hair. He was impeccably dressed. He smiled at Samuel and said, "Well, young man, are you coming in?"

Samuel realized he was half in and half out. He stepped in, closed the door, and then turned to the old man.

"Good mornin', sir. My name is Detective Samuel Hinton. I'm hopin' you can help me, sir."

The old man perched himself on a stool behind the counter. "Richard Sterling, at your service. Take a seat and tell me what you're looking for, young man."

Samuel did just that, as he sat looking at the multitudinous display of canisters lining the wall behind Mr. Sterling.

"Sir, I need to pick your brain." Samuel laid the folded square of linen on the counter. "Can you tell me anything about these?"

The old man picked up one of the butts and said, "May I open this?"

"Certainly, sir, whatever you need to do."

Samuel sat patiently as the old man extracted a small penknife from a pocket inside his waistcoat.

Sterling held the butt in his palm and carefully slit open the thin paper holding the small pinch of tobacco. He laid the knife down and just sat looking at the dark shreds of leaves. He used a fingertip to spread them across his palm, and then he sniffed. And sniffed again.

He raised his head and looked at Samuel for a moment. "I can tell you I don't have anything like this in my inventory. If it is what I think it is, I can probably order it for you. It would be coming from Louisiana."

"Can you tell me if you have ordered this for anyone in the past, sir?"

The old man shook his head. "No, young man, I have never had a request for it, and have only smelled it once before. If I'm correct, it is a blend the Choctaw Indians used to make, called Perique. To my knowledge, it is now only grown, and cured, in St. James Parrish. They use a unique pressing method. I personally have not smoked it, but I understand it has a distinct flavor of figs, with undertones of pepper. You may have detected the strong fruity aroma."

Samuel stared at the linen square on the counter for a long while. Mr. Sterling finally cleared his throat loudly to get his attention.

"Did you hear me, young man?"

"I'm sorry, sir. My mind was elsewhere. Do you know who we would contact in St. James Parrish if we wanted to get information about this tobacco?"

"I'm sorry; I don't have a particular name to give you. I just know it is unique to St. James Parrish."

"Sir, I know a great deal more now than I did before, so you have been very helpful."

The old man looked up at Samuel for a long moment. "I don't suppose you'd care to tell me why this blend is so important to you?"

Samuel stood and shook the old man's hand. "Well, I'm not about to take up smoking, if that's what you mean. I thank you again, sir, for the information, and your time."

The old man stared at the door for long minutes after Samuel left. Interesting young man, he thought. Very tight-lipped, but interesting.

Samuel finished writing his report and gathered his coat to head home. He had been going nonstop since three this morning, and he figured a hot meal and a warm bed would make for a good night's sleep. He gave a passing thought to stopping in to check on Kathleen Campbell. No, it might seem a little too forward, since he had no new information to give her. Maybe he would visit this weekend, just to be neighborly, since she had no family or friends in town.

Chapter Three

It was Saturday morning, and as Samuel walked through the kitchen door he could hear Charlotte's little voice begging Cook for custard for breakfast. Just the sound of her voice made him smile. As soon as she caught sight of him, she started squealing.

"Unc' Sammy, can I please have custard, please, please?"

Samuel scooped the little beauty up and twirled her around. "And did we ask Mama for custard?" Samuel could see it on her face; she was weighing the consequences of lying against the taste of warm custard. Her face fell, and he grinned; the consequences had won out.

"No, but she won't mind." Then she turned those blue eyes, with their long black lashes, on him. "You could have some too." She smiled.

"Well, it is mighty kind of you to share your custard with me, but I had my mouth all set for"—he glanced at Cook, who held up a plate of thick pancakes—"pancakes and bacon, and I'd be happy to share with you."

"Oh," she squealed, "pancakes, with lots of honey?"

"Yep, straight from Uncle Cyrus's bees. Let's wash up and then go to the dining room."

As Samuel perched her on the kitchen counter and

helped her wash her hands, he reflected on a future when he would have his own little princess to love. He suddenly envisioned a little girl with green eyes and unruly red curls. Whoa! Where did that come from? He shook his head and lowered Charlotte to the floor.

"Mama," she cried, as Mae entered the kitchen, "Unc' Sammy and me are havin' pancakes, and honey from the bees." She ran to her mother and threw both arms around her legs, looked up with a heart-melting smile, and asked, "You want some too, Mama?"

"Well, I might be persuaded. Your papa is having coffee with Grandpa. Why don't you run to the dining room and tell them what we're having?"

She could be heard all through the lower floor. "Papa, Papa, we're having pancakes."

Mae shook her head. "I'm raising a little heathen." Laughing, she turned to Samuel, and the smile faded away. She walked over and hugged her brother.

"Good morning, dear. Did you get some sleep last night?"

Samuel could hear the worry in her voice. She did not need to be worrying about him. She was five months along with her second child.

"I'm fine, Sister. Got all caught up on my sleep."

"I dreamed about you last night. It was the strangest thing. You were sitting on the porch of a lovely little home, and you were holding the most adorable little redheaded girl on your lap."

Samuel had been taking a sip of the coffee Cook had handed him, and he almost strangled.

"Oh, are you okay?" Mae pounded on his back.

"I will be if you'll stop beating me," he coughed out. "It just went down the wrong pipe."

He was not going to open a can of worms this morning. His sister would never let it rest until she met the girl in question, and he was not sure he was ready for the "inquisition."

Breakfast was a boisterous affair, but no one minded. Samuel looked around the table at all the people he loved. Papa and Eleanor might have met late in their lives, but you could still see the spark when they looked at each other.

Mae and her husband, Dr. Edward Finch, had fallen deeply in love the first day they met, six years ago now. Edward had his practice in town but also ministered to Mae's "girls."

That was what everyone called the women and children who made their way to Mae's village. Mae housed them, fed them, and educated them, and helped the Lord heal them, both spiritually and physically.

Samuel was so proud of his sister. She had not only survived a sexual assault, she had thrived. She had used her fear and anger to strengthen her faith in the Lord; then she had funneled that strength into her village for abused women. She'd built homes, a school, and a store where the women could sell their canned goods and sewn items. Many had come and were healed, then moved on as stronger human beings, thanks to Mae's care.

Then there were Cyrus and Patrick. Eleanor's pride and joy, Patrick, had just turned fourteen. He had followed after Cyrus like a lovable puppy for the last six years. They had raised prize-winning steers and rare breeds of chickens, and grown enough fresh vegetables for the family's use and for Mae's girls to sell. Cyrus was now attending the university, working toward a degree in agriculture. Samuel had no doubt that Patrick would follow, in time.

Samuel looked at the empty chair at the table. It had been two years now, and still he missed Hansu. He would come across a problem and have to stop himself from calling out to the little Chinaman. Hansu had been with his family since before Mae was born, and to hear his Papa tell it, the little man had been "older than dirt" when he came to them. He had passed peacefully in his sleep. A broken-hearted Cyrus had found him. He'd been given a place of honor in the family cemetery, and on occasion, when Samuel needed time alone, he would ride Zeus out to the cemetery, sit down, and carve whatever the current piece was while he talked with Hansu.

As breakfast wound down, Samuel turned to Eleanor. "If you're going into the shop this morning, I could run you in and fetch you home later."

"Yes, I need to go in until about one, and it would save your papa having to run around for me."

Garth Hinton looked at his son. "Are you working today, son?"

"I just need to look over some reports turned in late yesterday evening, sir. I can do that, then swing by and pick up Eleanor."

Garth was aware that Samuel was under some pressure to find the man who had killed the schoolteacher. He also knew that Samuel would not truly rest until the killer was found. Those closest to him could tell when he was on the hunt. There was a haunted look in his eyes, a restlessness that sleep could not curb. The boy had a gift, if you wanted to call it that. But sometimes that gift was hard to bear.

"That's fine, son, if it's not an inconvenience."

Eleanor smiled at Samuel. "Just give me a minute to gather my things, and I'll meet you out front."

The morning sun was warming the clear air, and it was going to be a beautiful day. Eleanor turned to Samuel. "Dear, I know you are wrapped up in a serious case, but please try to remember to eat, and get enough rest, and most of all be safe."

Samuel smiled down at the little woman who made his papa so happy. "Yes, ma'am, I promise I'll try to do better."

She laughed out loud. "All right, I know I sounded like I was speaking to Patrick, and I'm sorry for that, but you know Mae and I worry about you."

Samuel sobered up. "I know you do, and I'm grateful for that, but I wish Mae wouldn't worry so much, especially now, what with the baby and all. That reminds me. I don't want either of you, or any of the servants, or Mae's girls, going anywhere alone. I think the village is safe. I know that Roxanne and Mrs. Peters are crack shots, and the others can hold their own, but I won't rest easy until we find this man."

"Well, don't fret over me. Mae has her little beauty, and I have mine."

She opened her reticule, and Samuel could see the pistol his papa had insisted she carry after the Campbell woman had been found.

It was a sad statement, that all of Mae's girls were trained to handle a gun soon after their arrival at the village. But Samuel could at least tell himself he had done all he could to keep them safe. A few of them would eventually drift back to the type of abusive relationships they had run from, but for the most part, the women left stronger and wiser, and able to look forward to the type of life they had dreamed of as little girls.

****

Samuel dropped Eleanor off at her stylish shop and drove to headquarters. He'd already read all the reports submitted by the officers who'd canvassed the area near Mary Elizabeth's cottage. Hers was the only home for a mile stretch, before the lane merged with the main east-west road. He now had to check for anything in the area of Holmes and Maple, where he had found the cigarette butts.

Samuel was worried. Mama never visited unless it was necessary. If she said "another one is in danger," then he needed to find this man quickly. Samuel finally pushed back his chair. He had spent two hours sifting through reports with no new information. He needed a break to clear his head, and he had an idea just what would work.

Kathleen Campbell was sitting on the porch in a white rocking chair, sipping tea, when Samuel pulled up to the little picket fence. She carefully set her teacup on the table and stood.

"Good morning, Kathleen. How are you settling in?"

She tried to ignore the flutter in her stomach. "Fine, thank you, Samuel. Would you care for a cup of tea?"

"No, but thank you. I thought I'd stop by and see if you needed anything."

"That's very kind of you. I will need to find a market, and pick up a few things for the kitchen. And some ice for the icebox."

Samuel shared his slow almost-smile. "Well, then,

you're in luck. I know the perfect place. If you wouldn't mind the company, I can take you to the Ladies' Village Emporium. I happen to know the owners, and they have everything you might need, from hand-stitched bedding to fresh baked bread."

A few minutes later, she was seated in the motorcar. "So tell me about this Emporium. You say you know the owners?"

Samuel smiled, "Well, it's quite a story, but the long and short of it is that my sister opened a home for women who need a little help. She makes sure they get an education and are trained in some sort of skill that can help them earn a living. They sell their crafts, canned goods, and fresh vegetables in the Emporium and can earn a wage that way."

"How kind of her. Samuel, I must know. Do you have any new information for me? Are you any closer to finding my sister's killer?"

Samuel was sorry to see the smile had left her face. He accepted that he enjoyed seeing that smile, and he wanted to be the one to bring it back. He reached out and covered her hand with his, where it rested on the seat between them.

"No, Kathleen, I'm sorry. There is no news, but I promise you, it is only a matter of time. I will not give up." He squeezed her hand. "The minute I know something, I will let you know, but until then, you need to put it aside and allow yourself a rest from your grief. We fix those things we can, and then we'd best let the Lord handle the rest."

Kathleen looked into those golden eyes, filled with compassion, and wondered how a man this sensitive could perform the job he was engaged in. She gave him a weak smile. "Good advice. I am a believer in the power of prayer, but sometimes I need to pray for patience."

Samuel chuckled. "Well that certainly makes you human. I don't think there's a person amongst us who doesn't try to pressure the Lord sometimes."

Samuel was nosing the motorcar off the road in front of a well-kept store with a large window. Kathleen could see mannequins of all sizes in the window. Samuel opened the door and took her hand as she stepped from the car. He smiled. "Welcome to the Emporium."

As soon as they stepped inside, the aroma of fresh-baked bread enveloped them. Kathleen observed shelves lined with jars of canned fruits and vegetables on one side, and racks of brightly colored clothing of all sizes on the opposite wall. There were groups of kitchen utensils, bed linens, handmade baskets, and endless other craft items on display in the center aisles. Everything was sparkling clean and well organized.

There was a shout, and then a blond-haired imp about ten years old flew around a display. The whirlwind threw himself at Samuel's legs. Samuel reached down, grabbed the imp, and hung him upside down for a few seconds before returning the now giggling bundle to the floor.

"Did you make me something, huh, Uncle Samuel, did you bring me a new horse, huh, did you?" The little blond boy was jumping from one foot to the other when a smiling woman grabbed him by the collar and turned to them.

"Good day, miss. Welcome to the Emporium. Samuel, you can explain to this young lady why my child is behavin' like a heathen in public. Jimmy, stop making a spectacle of yourself, and let them at least get in the door."

"Good mornin', Emma. How's business today?" Samuel turned to Kathleen. "Kathleen, this is Emma Rogers. She manages the Emporium, and this young man is her son, Jimmy. He manages to stay out of trouble for the most part. Emma, this is Miss Kathleen Campbell. She is taking over the primary school for the rest of the school year."

Emma immediately sobered. This must be the sister of the young woman who was killed. She took Kathleen's extended hand. "Miss, your sister was a lovely girl. She shopped here often. If there is anything we can do, or anything you need, please don't hesitate to ask."

Kathleen's eyes filled as she nodded, and Emma could see she was struggling to hold back the pain. "Well, miss, I'll leave you to your shopping, and I'll just take this young'un off your hands. Samuel, if you need anything, let me know."

Young Jimmy struggled for only a moment as his mother led him away by the ear. Samuel grinned. Jimmy was a good boy. He'd had a rough start in life. His mother had come to Mae's village when he was only four years old. Both of them had been covered in bruises and looked half starved. They had barely begun to recover when the man they'd run from had come looking for them. He'd come to drag them back, and Mae had stopped him. She had sent him on his way with a bullet in the arm and a warning to never come back. They had always suspected he'd been the one to burn down the lumber storage yard for the village.

Kathleen turned to Samuel and caught the fond smile on his face. "So you are his uncle?"

"No, I was just the first man to ever be kind to him, and he just sort of latched onto me, him and about a dozen more."

She smiled. "So you like children? Do you have any of your own?"

Samuel looked into those green eyes and considered a moment before answering. "I've always known marriage and a family are in my future. I just haven't had reason to think much about it before now."

Kathleen had to drag her gaze away from his compelling eyes. She could feel the heat of her blush. "Well, I had better start shopping. I'm taking up way too much of your day, sir."

She picked up a basket and headed for the produce at the back of the store. He hadn't meant to embarrass her. It was the truth; he hadn't given much thought to the future. He'd always known that the Lord would send him a mate when the time was right. He was twenty-four, he had a good job, and he loved kids. He grinned to himself. Heck, maybe the time was right now.

They loaded Kathleen's supplies and were leaving the parking area when Samuel spoke. "I hope you don't mind, but I need to run by Taylor's and pick up my stepmother. She only works a half day on Saturday, so I drove her in this morning and will be taking her home."

"Please, you have been so kind, you do what you need to do, and I'll be fine."

Samuel smiled. "You'll love Eleanor; everyone does. She is the second best thing that ever happened to my father, and we all love her dearly."

Kathleen was surprised when they stopped in front of Taylor's. This was the kind of establishment she would expect to see in a place like Boston.

Samuel stepped around the motorcar and opened her door as he smiled down at her. "Come on, you know you want to see the inside. All those woman things are just calling your name."

Kathleen laughed at his foolishness, and the sound warmed his insides.

The little bell over the door announced their presence, and a soft voice called out, "Be with you in just a moment."

The beautiful fabrics and hats on display overwhelmed Kathleen. She had yet to find a hat that could tame her wild mane of curls, but she so enjoyed searching for one.

Eleanor came bustling through the curtain hiding the dressing rooms. She stopped short at the sight of the beautiful woman looking at the hats. She looked at Samuel with an eyebrow raised in question. He smiled broadly.

"Are you about finished for the day?"

Kathleen turned when he spoke. She was facing a lovely, small woman, with red-gold hair that had just the beginnings of white at the temples. She couldn't have been much more than five feet tall and was immaculately dressed in a beautiful, peach-colored blouse and dark brown skirt.

Samuel smiled at the unspoken curiosity in Eleanor's eyes. "Eleanor, this is Kathleen Campbell. She will be the primary school teacher for the remainder of this year. Kathleen, this is Eleanor Hinton, my much-loved stepmother."

Eleanor turned a lovely shade of pink. "Oh, hush, you silly goose. It's nice to meet you, dear. Please excuse Samuel. He loves to tease me."

"Kathleen just got into town day before yesterday and needed a few things, so I offered to take her to the Emporium. We'll be dropping her off on our way home."

Kathleen could plainly see the love between these two. It warmed her heart but saddened her at the same time. As a child, she had often wished her family had been more open in their feelings for each other. As a grown woman, she had wondered if this lack of intimacy was what had led her sister to leave home at an early age. Mary Elizabeth had left immediately after receiving her teaching degree. She had signed on as a relief teacher and had been in several states in the past five years. As Mary Elizabeth moved into each new position, their mother would say, "Maybe this time she will find a man and settle down." But Kathleen had never believed it. Her sister had been perfectly content with the solitary life.

Kathleen listened to the banter between Eleanor and Samuel as they drove. They spoke of a Cyrus and his garden, a Mae and a Charlotte, and how Charlotte had charmed her father into a puppy for her birthday. They were describing the kind of loving family she had always dreamed of having one day.

They made a short stop at the icehouse and then proceeded to the cottage. When Samuel stopped the motorcar, Eleanor turned to Kathleen.

"Dear, if you don't have any plans for this afternoon, why don't you come home with us and share supper? It is a family gathering, and there's always room for one more. We would love to have you."

"That's very kind of you, but I can't intrude." Kathleen was already regretting her answer when Samuel walked round to open her door.

"Well, you won't be intruding, so hand me those baskets. We'll get them inside, and you can grab a wrap for when it cools off this evening."

Eleanor eyed the two as they entered the cottage. She couldn't wait for Mae to see this. Samuel had been born with a need to protect all women, young and old, but there was something different about this one. She wasn't just someone to be protected. She might be someone to love.

Chapter Four

Cyrus and Patrick were chasing a young goat around the yard when Samuel eased into the circular drive at the front of the manor. A very dirty Charlotte was clapping her hands and giggling uncontrollably.

Eleanor shook her head. "Kathleen, welcome to our home."

Samuel got out and rushed around to open their doors. "Kathleen, make a run for the front door with Eleanor, and I'll try to keep the goat and the giggling heathen from getting you dirty."

Martha Patrick, the head housekeeper, met them in the front hallway. "Saints preserve us! Did I just see a goat chase you in?"

Eleanor sighed. "Yes, you did. It seems Charlotte has been up to mischief again." She turned to Kathleen. "Charlotte is Mae and Edward's daughter. She loves to turn the animals loose and then be entertained by her uncles trying to catch them."

Martha shook her head. "Here, miss, let me take your wrap. I have tea on, and Cook has some lovely-looking tarts cooling in the kitchen."

"That sounds wonderful, Martha. Is Mae in the back parlor?" Eleanor asked.

"Yes, ma'am. The doctor told her to go rest, just before he drove out to the village to check on the new little one."

Eleanor smiled at Kathleen. "Come along, dear. We will have a few minutes' peace and quiet before Samuel has Charlotte presentable and brings her in."

Kathleen followed Eleanor through the wide hall. The manor was much larger than she had expected. It seemed such a grand place, and it had been a little disconcerting to see young men chasing animals on the front lawn. This family was certainly a lively bunch.

They entered a large sitting room at the rear of the house, and Kathleen's gaze was immediately drawn to the stately piano at the back of the room. It was a beautiful piece. It was only after taking it in that she noticed the dark-haired woman reclining on a sofa.

Eleanor stopped beside the sofa and spoke softly. "Mae, are you asleep, dear?"

"No, just enjoying the peace and quiet." The woman sat up and smiled. Then she caught sight of Kathleen. "Good golly Moses, why didn't you tell me we had company?"

Kathleen smiled. "Please, don't get up on my account." It was plain to see the woman was pregnant.

Mae shot a questioning look at Eleanor. "Mae, this is Kathleen Campbell. She is a friend of Samuel's."

Now she had Mae's full attention.

"Oh, no, we're not friends, I mean...we are...I mean, we just met." By now Mae was really interested. The woman was blushing a very becoming pink and seemed to have run out of words.

Eleanor took pity on Kathleen. "Kathleen's sister was our schoolteacher, dear. She is going to finish out the year for us. Samuel took her shopping at the Emporium today, and I find no reason for her to be sitting in the cottage alone all day, when she could come and be entertained by goat-chasing farmers and curly-haired heathens."

"Oh, no!" Mae exclaimed. "Did Charlotte turn the goat loose again?"

Martha answered from the doorway as she entered with the teacart. "She most certainly did. Her favorite uncle has her in the kitchen right now, lecturing her on what is and is not acceptable behavior for a little lady, all while he is attempting to wash a half acre of dirt from her hands and face."

Eleanor was trying to hide a smile. "Kathleen, please have a seat. The show has only just begun."

Mae nodded her agreement. "I could probably call this a circus and sell tickets." She grinned ruefully.

"Kathleen, as you can see, we are very informal. Please help yourself to a cup of tea and a fruit tart. Cook makes the best mayhaw tarts for fifty miles in any direction," Eleanor said. She passed a cup of tea and a tart to Mae.

Mae waited until Kathleen had tea and tart in hand before she asked, "Kathleen, have you been a teacher long?"

"No, I graduated from Simmons College for Women two years ago. My sister, Mary Elizabeth, left home almost five years ago now, and our mother had a very hard time accepting that. So once I graduated, in order to stay closer to home I took a position as tutor to the daughters of a vice president of the Porter Motor Company. They were sweet girls. This past September, I escorted them to New York, where they will be attending the Finch School. It is a finishing school for young women. Their father wanted them to be prepared properly for marrying into society. I had only been home from New York City a couple of weeks when we received word of Mary Elizabeth's death."

"Your sister was a dear woman. I spoke with her at length one afternoon when she was shopping in the Emporium. I was working on convincing her to come visit with my girls, at the village. I was hoping to have her come out every other Saturday and teach history." Mae took a sip of her tea.

"History and geography were her favorite subjects. She loved tracing the roots of different areas; how they were settled, and by whom."

Before Kathleen could continue, a now almost-clean Charlotte burst through the parlor door.

"Mama, I clean now. Can I have a tart and milk? Please, please, Mama?"

A grinning Samuel was right behind her. He had a smudge of dirt on his left jaw and another on his shirt pocket.

"I did the best I could. At least her hands and face are passable, now."

Charlotte ran to the sideboard and took out a linen tablecloth. She returned to her mother's chair and spread the cloth on the floor.

"See, Mama?" She smiled sweetly. "I be careful. No tart on the chair." She promptly sat on the cloth, crossed her legs, and smoothed her dress over her scuffed knees before folding her hands and waiting patiently for someone to serve her.

Mae rose from her chair and handed Charlotte a tart and the glass of milk that Martha had included on the cart. "All right, little missy, you know the rules. You must stay on the cloth, do not interrupt the grownups, and clean up after yourself. Understood?"

"Yes, ma'am," was the sweet answer, and the child stuffed a piece of tart into her mouth as soon as the words were out.

Samuel had taken the seat beside Kathleen. "I promised you would not be intruding. When I've finished my tea, I'll show you around. I assure you the goat has been secured."

Samuel turned to Mae and asked about Cyrus's plans for next year's garden. As they spoke, Kathleen was free to look around the parlor. Her eyes kept straying to the piano in the corner. It looked like an early Baldwin model. She had learned to play on one of those. She was so intent on the instrument that it took her a moment to realize Samuel had spoken to her.

"I'm sorry, could you repeat that?"

"I said do you play the piano?"

"Yes." She smiled tentatively. "I've had some training."

He smiled broadly. "Then you will have to play for us after supper." He drained his teacup and stood. He held out his hand and smiled down at her. "Come, we'll take a walk around the grounds. You can tell me about Boston."

Charlotte jumped up, knocking over her glass that, fortunately, she had drained. "Wait for me, Unc' Samuel!"

Mae grabbed her as she darted by. "Oh, no, little missy, you have to have a real bath, and a nap, before your papa gets home, or else you won't be able to sit in his lap when he reads to you."

Charlotte loved her uncle, but she adored her papa.

"Yes, Mama, I needs a bath."

Samuel presented Kathleen with the sweater she

had given over to Martha earlier. Eleanor and Mae exchanged a look.

"I may take Kathleen over to see the village. We'll be back by suppertime."

Samuel opened one of the French doors and led Kathleen out toward the lake.

"So." Eleanor grinned. "What do you think of that?"

Mae shook her head slowly. "I'm not sure what to think. Is that my same brother who left here this morning? That is the most talkative I've ever seen him."

"I couldn't believe it when they showed up at the shop. And then when we got her home, he refused to let her decline the invitation to supper. I think our Samuel is very interested."

Mae shook her head in wonder. "She is a beauty and seems very nice. Oh! My gosh! I forgot all about it," Mae exclaimed.

"About what?"

Mae turned to Eleanor with a look of disbelief on her face. "The dream," she said. "I dreamed Samuel was sitting on the front porch of a little house. He was holding a beautiful little girl with the curliest red hair I had ever seen."

Eleanor was still for a moment. She began to chuckle, then laughed until she had to use her napkin to dry her eyes.

****

Kathleen stood looking out toward the lake. "This is a beautiful spot for a home."

"The lady who left it all to Mae had a great love for this land. Mae has tried to keep that same feeling alive in her village. She tries to keep the place warm and welcoming to all the women who pass through."

"What part did you play in this village?" Kathleen turned those clear green eyes on Samuel.

"Oh, I made a few pieces of furniture for the houses. Not much, really," he replied.

"Somehow I doubt that. You seem very close to your sister and her family."

He did not want to remind her of her loss, so he changed the subject. "Come, let me show you what is important to me."

Samuel led Kathleen to the barn. They entered through the side door, and she could immediately smell lemon oil.

Samuel led her to a large piece of canvas spread on the floor of the barn. There was a two-drawer escritoire standing in the middle of the canvas. It had thin, dainty legs with carved vines running up to the drawers. The drawer fronts had carved roses. The piece was made of red maple, with a beautiful sheen from the oil Samuel had applied in light coats, massaging the oil into the delicate carvings.

Kathleen raised questioning eyes to Samuel. "Good heavens, did you make this?"

Samuel tried not to look too pleased. "Yes, it's what I do to relax. Since I was a small boy, I've loved the feel of wood in my hands. And it didn't hurt that my father owned a sawmill."

"Oh, Samuel, this is beautiful. You obviously have a gift," Kathleen almost whispered.

"Give me your hand."

Kathleen looked at him questioningly as she held out her hand to him.

Samuel paused while holding her hand. He marveled at the softness of it, and was distracted for a moment. He looked into her eyes and asked, "Do you like surprises?"

She answered him softly, "I guess that depends on the surprise."

Samuel guided her hand to the rose on the top left side of the drawer. He used the tip of her index finger to stroke the flower and a petal slid aside to show a small recess in the flower.

The look of surprise and delight on her face was like a balm to Samuel's heart. He had no idea why it was so important to him to make her smile. His heart just wanted to see those eyes shining with joy.

"How did you do that?" she asked.

Samuel smiled slowly. "A man can't be expected to give up all his secrets the first time a woman asks, now can he?"

Kathleen laughed out loud. "It's not like I'm going to steal your trade secrets." She sobered and said, "But truly, you are a gifted craftsman. This is a beautiful piece of work."

"Thank you. I'm glad you like it. Now, let's go have a look at the village."

They drove out to the main road, and then another mile to the west. Before Kathleen was a group of four neat homes. Each had a friendly-looking front porch with rocking chairs, and potted plants hanging from the railings. There was a larger central building, and a little, blonde girl and two older boys playing under an oak tree at the edge of the lawns. As soon as the children heard the motorcar, they jumped up and started running. Samuel barely made it out of the vehicle before the three threw themselves at him. Kathleen smiled as the little girl wrapped herself around one of his long legs. He grabbed a boy up under each arm and swung the giggling bodies around. Kathleen had to laugh; this man drew children like flies to honey. She let herself out of the vehicle and started around it.

A little gray-haired woman stepped out onto the porch of one of the houses and yelled, "Samuel Hinton, those boys just had a big lunch. Don't be wallerin' them all over the place unless you want 'em to share it with you."

Samuel started peeling off children as he called back, "Yes, ma'am, I promise I'll behave."

He turned, held out his hand to Kathleen, and introduced her to the children before he added, "Come, there's someone else I want you to meet." She paused for a second and then placed her hand in his as they walked toward the little woman.

"Mrs. Peters, this is Kathleen Campbell. She is our new schoolteacher in town. Kathleen, this is Mrs. Peters. She makes the best pies and cobblers in four counties."

The little woman blushed like a schoolgirl. "Samuel Hinton, how many times have I told you not to exaggerate?"

Samuel and Kathleen spent nearly an hour visiting with Mrs. Peters. She had been the Hinton men's housekeeper when Mae left for Tallahassee. She was full of stories of the boy's shenanigans that kept Kathleen laughing.

Samuel found he could face the embarrassment of the stories as long as it kept that smile on Kathleen's face. He finally stood, extended a hand to Kathleen, and said, "All right, enough of that. None of those stories can ever leave here. I have a reputation as a hard-nosed officer of the law to keep up."

Kathleen was still smiling, as the "hard-nosed lawman" hugged the little woman and promised to come back soon.

He made eye contact with Kathleen as they drove away. She was still smiling. "All right, don't make me regret taking you there," he growled.

"Oh, I'm afraid the secret is out now. The big tough lawman is mush inside," she teased.

Samuel just shook his head. They returned to the manor and spent another two hours with the Hintons and the Finches. After supper, they all moved to the back parlor to relax. Kathleen asked Mae, "Do you play the piano?"

Mae shook her head sadly. "No, it belonged to Lady Wellington. When Charlotte gets a little older, I hope to have lessons for her, though. How did you learn to play?"

Kathleen smiled. "My mother was a music teacher in her younger days. Both Mary Elizabeth and I have played since we were Charlotte's age."

"Oh, would you please play for us? We would love to hear something."

At everyone's encouragement, Kathleen walked to the piano. She sat still for a moment, closed her eyes, and then started to play.

Samuel was hypnotized watching Kathleen. She swayed a little, as her slender hands danced over the keys. Her eyes stayed closed, and Samuel wondered what memories whispered through her mind as she filled the room with such beautiful sounds.

When she had finished the haunting melody, there was a deep silence in the room, finally broken by Charlotte's little voice, "Do it again, please? Do it again!"

Everyone laughed, and then begged for another song. Kathleen blushed sweetly, but Samuel could see that her eyes held tears that were threatening to spill.

He stood and said, "We'll have to have her play for us another time. Right now I have to get her back to town." He already had Kathleen's sweater in hand.

She thanked everyone for welcoming her, made her goodbyes, and Samuel had her out the front door in no time.

He got her seated in the motorcar, then gently placed a thin quilt across her lap. After sliding in behind the wheel, he turned to Kathleen. "Are you all right?"

She gave him a weak smile, and he could see that one of the tears had escaped, leaving a trail down her cheek. He gently cupped her chin in his large hand and wiped the tear away with his thumb. "It was the piano music, right?"

She nodded. "That was one of Mary Elizabeth's favorites." She took his hand in hers. "Thank you so much for today. You have a remarkable family, and their love for each other is so apparent."

Samuel squeezed her hand gently. "If it suits your fancy, there could be many more days like today."

Kathleen was glad dusk had descended and her face was in shadow. She wasn't sure it was seemly for a woman to be so transparent. This man evoked feelings in her that only one other had been able to stir. Kathleen considered this as they drove in silence.

Several men had courted her. Her father was a wealthy, established businessman, and while a dowry was an old-fashioned idea, some had approached her with the intent of bettering themselves. She had attended soirees and church suppers with first one and then another gentleman. She had never encouraged any of them until James Sheridan entered her life. Sheridan was her father's right-hand man in Boston. He was educated, handsome, and a heart breaker. Maybe she'd been a little naïve to think a man of his caliber would be so taken with her charms that he would defy her father. When her father learned she had lost her heart to an underling, he had offered James a position in the London offices, and the man had jumped at the chance. It had taken Kathleen quite some time to regain her self-esteem after losing out to a big office in London.

Admittedly, sometimes her tongue was sharp, and she did not suffer fools gladly. But Samuel, to put it simply, was different. She was used to men who were formally educated, who moved in society's upper circles, and who had ambition. While Samuel showed none of these qualities, he showed deep insight into others, without being arrogant. He seemed to be comfortable with the position in life he had created for himself.

They reached the cottage, and Samuel said, "Give me your key, and I'll get the door and light a lamp." She handed him the large key and waited in the motorcar until the windows filled with light. When she entered, Samuel was kneeling at the hearth, lighting the logs he had just placed in the grate. How could the simple act of lighting a fire arouse her so? A warmth spread through her that had nothing to do with the fire.

Samuel stood. "That should take…" He had been about to say the fire would take care of the chill, but when he saw the look on Kathleen's face, he lost his voice. Their eyes locked, and he was at her side in three long strides. He reached past her shoulder and shoved the door closed.

Kathleen wanted to speak, but her mind had shut down.

Samuel placed a hand on each side of her face and slowly lowered his mouth to hers. Her eyes closed long before their lips met.

Samuel raised his face and whispered, "Kathleen, open your eyes. I want to see your soul."

She was so weak with longing for something unknown that she leaned into him to keep from falling. Her eyes opened, and she had the look of a drunkard. "Please," she whispered.

"Please, what?"

She closed her eyes again, and as she slipped both arms around his firm body, she said, "Please don't stop."

Samuel groaned as if in actual pain as he buried his face in her hair and wrapped her in a crushing embrace. "Good golly Moses, woman," he moaned. "What are you doing to me?" He placed searing kisses on her throat as she clung to him.

She whimpered, and suddenly Samuel stopped. "Oh, Lord, Kathleen, I'm sorry. Did I hurt you?"

He took her by the shoulders and put space between them. He couldn't let go of her—she was too weak to stand on her own.

She finally opened her eyes. They slowly filled with tears. "No, you didn't hurt me. It was just so…

Samuel, what is happening?"

He gave a tortured laugh. "Honey, I was fifteen feet from a lightning strike once and wasn't this scared. Here, sit down, and I'll get you a glass of water." He lowered her to the settee and strode to the kitchen. Through the doorway, she could see him brace himself on the edge of the sink and take several long, deep breaths. His hands seemed to tremble as he tried to grip the handle of the pump.

When he got back to the front parlor, Kathleen was right where he had left her. She had both arms wrapped around a plump embroidered pillow. He knelt by the settee, slowly took the pillow from her hands, and replaced it with the glass. "Here, love, drink this."

Kathleen drank deeply, and the cool water helped soothe her nerves. She took a deep breath and met his eyes.

"Better?" he asked, smiling weakly.

Kathleen nodded yes, but answered, "No. I've never had this sort of reaction to a kiss before. I'm not a schoolgirl anymore, and I have been kissed by several men."

Samuel stood slowly and breathed deeply for a few seconds.

"I don't want to hear about any other kisses you may have known, but maybe you should give it some consideration. I mean, why it's different this time. I'm going to go now and give you some time to think."

Katherine stood quickly—a little too quickly, and had to close her eyes to still the spinning room.

Samuel extended a hand to steady her, but was careful not to get too close. Perhaps he, like herself, had already used just about all of his self-control.

She slowly opened her eyes. "Thank you, that's better. I'm sorry, I…"

Samuel placed his fingertips on her soft lips. "Shh, don't apologize. I'm the one who should be sorry for taking advantage of your emotional state. But I can't seem to say 'sorry' for something that seemed so right. So I'm going home, and you are going to lock this door behind me, get some rest, and do some thinking."

Kathleen wanted to talk about this thing between them, but he turned and closed the door behind him.

Chapter Five

Hamish McDuff was a good businessman. He made a fair living from the ale he produced. His most requested recipe was one his granddad had passed down to him as a young boy, for a dark, rich brew. With the cry of "prohibition" going on in Georgia, and the Florida laws testing "what is and is not an intoxicating" drink, his moneymaker, so to speak, was kept very low key. That would be the "white lightning." Oh, you didn't just ask the barkeep for this special treat. It was made without benefit of the payout to the taxman. Hamish didn't brew it himself, as he had no desire to run amok of the law. But that didn't stop him from buying it from those who cared not one whit about taxes, or the law. Like the huge fellow unloading several earthenware jars this very moment.

Hamish didn't even know the man's name. But as dependable as the turning of the earth, during the dark of the moon each month this great hulking beast of a man would show up with the liquid fire that the tavern keepers had come to expect from Hamish. The man was at least twenty stone, and so tall he had to duck to get in the door of the storehouse. He could carry a small barrel full of ale under each arm and not miss a breath. He would unload his wagon in the late night hours and be long gone before daybreak.

Tonight there was a woman with him. She sat

unmoving on the wagon seat. She kept her shawl-covered head down and never made a sound.

Hamish could not help but wonder what type of woman could live in the swamp with a brute of a man like this one. One with hands the size of small hams, and who wore moccasins instead of boots.

The woman wanted to scream as the wagon rolled away into the black night, and only the rope tied round her ankle prevented her from escaping into that blackness. That and the fact that she had no doubt the man would kill her if she tried.

The man turned the wagon west again but took a different route. Although the woman was curious, she never opened her mouth. The wagon finally came to rest near a large dark building. There was no moon to shine off any windows, so the woman could not tell what the building was, or why they were stopping. The man disappeared into the darkness, and the only sound the woman detected was the soft creaking of boards. She had to admit, for so large a man, he melted into the darkness as soundlessly as a panther.

A few minutes later the man returned, just as quietly, and placed a small pouch in her lap. She knew better than to question him, and after a while her fingers detected the contents of the sack. Bullets. He must have stolen bullets from that building. She returned her attention to the road. She thought they were headed west again, just on a sidetrack, running parallel to the main road. They only passed one cottage, with its neat little fence, before they merged with the main road.

The wagon traveled west for hours, with no word spoken between the man and his captive. Occasionally it would hit a rock, and the jarring would cause the rope to rub on the woman's raw ankle. She wasn't sure how many months she had been with the man. It was at least a year, as she was approaching a second winter as his slave.

The whole thing was her own fault. She had been making enough to live on in Pensacola. It wasn't much of a living, but then what was an uneducated runaway from Georgia going to do? If she hadn't run when she had, she would have had to kill the uncle she'd been living with. He had been after her ever since she'd become a woman at thirteen. When her aunt passed on, she knew it would only be a matter of time. So she lit out one night and ended up in a brothel. For a while she just did laundry, and cooked a little, but there was no money to be made that way. At sixteen she'd ended up working on her back.

Then she'd learned about a woman in Tallahassee who was helping girls like her to put their lives back in order. She'd hitched a ride with a couple of farmers headed east. They'd used her and left her on the side of the road. And then he had showed up.

She convinced him to let her come on this trip, so she could memorize every tree and boulder along the way. This was her chance to get the lay of the land for when she made her run. And then he'd made her put a sack over her head for the first few miles. She could not tell where the wagon hit the main road. Oh, he believed she was all broken in now, 'cause she'd stopped fighting. He had beaten her so badly the last time, she'd been sure she was going to die. So she had started using her head, controlling her temper and planning.

It had been the clothes that pushed her over the edge. He'd come back from his last trip and thrown a dress and underclothes at her. As if he expected her to be grateful. They'd still had the woman's fragrance on them. And a few spatters of blood.

She needed at least one more month to build up her strength for the swim across the river. It would be a cold swim by the end of November, but she would make it. She had to. She was not alone anymore. She and the baby would live or die together. Her eighteen years on this earth had been of little note to anyone. But she could change that, if she could keep the baby alive. She could mold a life better than the one she had struggled through.

Chapter Six

Kathleen finished the letter to her mother. She had written all about the school, the twenty-six students, her nice little cottage, and Taylor's Millinery. She wished she and her mother had a closer relationship. Then she could have written about Samuel. She could have described his golden eyes, the strength in his hands, and the fire in his kiss. Well, maybe not that. She was used to keeping her feelings to herself. Even before Mary Elizabeth had left home, Kathleen was aware that they all existed in their own little worlds, taking care not to let one overlap into the others' lives.

After having spent time with Samuel's family, she was justified in believing hers was not a normal family. She had adjusted to this, and didn't really believe she was deprived, until she had seen Samuel interact with so many children. The joy on their faces, and his, had shown her just how much she had missed. And she did not want to miss any more.

Samuel had awakened a need for laughter and closeness. He had given her a glimpse of what it could be like to live in the moment and share it with others. Kathleen realized the most painful part of losing Mary Elizabeth was the realization that she was basically alone in the world. Meeting Samuel had given her the understanding that she did not want to live life that way. Oh, if she had stayed in Boston she would have eventually accepted some man's proposal, and her life would have fallen into the sad, lonely pattern set by her parents. She was now sure she could not accept that cold way of life. She had seen love and joy, concern and caring, and she wanted it for her very own.

****

Samuel was reading patrol reports when Edith Hampton stopped in front of his desk.

"You had a message from a Mr. Sterling. He says he has something for you."

Samuel closed the folder and sat back in his chair. "Did he say what?"

"No. Just that he would be closing at five this afternoon." Edith propped one hip on the corner of the desk. "So. Are we making any progress with the schoolteacher?"

Anger started to rise in him. "Edith, I am not going to discuss Kathleen with you."

"I was talking about the dead one," she snapped. "I don't want to know anything about your private life."

Samuel let out a long sigh. It was time to smother this, once and for all.

"Edith, have I ever treated you as anything other than a competent and accomplished secretary? Have I ever given you any reason to think our friendship was anything other than professional?"

Edith was standing now. "No, no, you have not. And I am beginning to understand that you never will." She paused and swallowed back another smart remark. "Samuel, we have worked together for almost three years, and I believed there was something more than business between us. Captain Lance spoke with me yesterday. I understand that I have let my personal

feelings create a less than ideal working atmosphere…"
Her voice trailed off as her eyes began to burn.

"Aww, Edith, please don't cry."

She swiped at her eyes, straightened her back, and conjured up a watery smile. "Don't worry. I'm not going to make a scene. I had time to think about this last night, and I understand that I created this problem myself. I'm sorry if it has caused you any embarrassment, and I assure you that it is over. From this moment forward, ours will be a good working relationship, and that is all." Edith turned and walked stiffly back down the hall to her desk.

Samuel figured it might be a good idea to go see Mr. Sterling now.

When he arrived at the tobacconist's shop, the old gentleman was just as dapper today as the first time Samuel had met him.

"Good afternoon, sir. I was told you had something for me."

Mr. Sterling's blue eyes twinkled. "Young man, you seemed so interested in the Perique tobacco, when last we met, that I proceeded to do a little study of it. I contacted a friend in Louisiana, who in turn contacted a member of the Poche family in St. James Parish. I was able to order a canister of the exclusive Perique blend, and I have a small pouch for you." The old gentleman placed a black drawstring pouch on the counter.

"Well, Mr. Sterling, that was mighty kind of you." Samuel smiled as he picked up the pouch, loosened the drawstring, and inhaled the aroma of the contents. "Yes, sir, that is definitely the same. A lot stronger, as it's fresh, but surely the same make-up."

Mr. Sterling returned Samuel's smile. "I don't

suppose you'd like to tell me now what this is all about?"

Samuel stood shook the old gentleman's leathered hand. "I thank you, sir. This may well come in handy for an investigation I'm working on." Samuel inquired the cost and paid it, then smiled again as he slipped the pouch into his coat pocket and headed out the door.

Mr. Sterling, observing Samuel as he walked away, chuckled to himself. "Well played, my boy, well played."

As Samuel strode back to headquarters, he made mental lists, aligning the things he did know on one side, and the things he didn't know on the other. He did not believe in coincidence, and there were too many things he did know to ignore them.

For instance, there were moccasin tracks at the scene. The killer was a very large man. The Acadians, along with the Choctaw and Chickasaw Indians, had originally produced Perique tobacco. Samuel was confident enough now to work up a profile on the killer and get it out to the public.

Samuel was climbing on his motorcycle when he remembered Mae had asked him to stop by the Emporium on the way home. Emma had some sewing supplies for the village.

Attacked by a squealing Jimmy as he entered the store, he hoisted the boy into the air for their usual roughhousing. Jimmy giggled and reached into Samuel's pocket.

"Did ya bring me another horse?" he asked, as Samuel swung him to the floor.

Jimmy's hand was jerked out of the pocket, and the pouch of tobacco came with it. The boy's eyes got round, and his body stilled. He stood frozen, a look of terror on his little face, until finally he threw the pouch to the floor as if it had been a rattlesnake and ran screaming to the storeroom.

Samuel was dumbfounded. He scooped up the pouch, put it back in his pocket, and slowly followed Jimmy. He found the boy, pale and shaking, in his mama's arms.

Emma was almost as pale as Jimmy and looked at Samuel questioningly.

"Samuel, are you alone? Is there someone outside?"

"No, Emma, it's just me. What's wrong with Jimmy? I know he's scared nigh to death, but why?"

The boy looked up at Samuel and whispered, "Where is he? You won't let him take Mama, will you?"

Samuel knelt and took the boy in his arms. "Jimmy, I don't know who you're talkin' about, but you know I would never let someone take your mama away."

Emma said, "Let's go upstairs where we can talk." She turned and climbed the staircase that led to the apartments above the store.

Samuel followed her, clutching a still trembling Jimmy to his broad chest.

Once they were seated in Emma's sitting room, the child relaxed his hold on Samuel.

Emma was visibly shaken, but she spoke clearly. "Samuel, do you have tobacco on you? I smell it."

"Well, yes, I do. But what…"

Emma interrupted him. "Where did you get it? Who did you get it from?"

"I got it from the tobacco shop, Emma. What's this all about?"

Emma smiled shakily at Jimmy. "See, sweetie, it's okay. He's not here, and we are safe. Do you believe your mama?"

Jimmy climbed down from Samuel's lap and put his arms around his mama. "I'm sorry, Mama, I didn't mean to scare you, but you always said if I thought he was near I should run."

"Yes, and you did well, sweetie. You did just what I told you to do, and I'm proud of you. Now, please go downstairs and tell Roxanne to give you that package of sewing things I wrapped up for Mae."

Samuel waited until the boy was out of earshot and then gave Emma a long look. "You wanna tell me what just happened?"

"I'm so sorry, Samuel, but when Jimmy said he was here, I panicked."

"Who, Emma? Who was here? Start at the beginning."

"Samuel, do you remember when Jimmy and I first showed up at Mae's village? Remember the day Mae had to shoot a man in the arm?"

"Well, of course I do. But what…" Samuel's voice trailed off, as his mind took him back to that day.

He and Pa had been at the manor when they heard a shot at the village. They didn't hear the second one because they were in the truck and flying there when it was fired. When they slid into the yard at the village, Mae was holding a man at gunpoint. The man was bleeding from his upper arm. Samuel sat very still while his mind played the scene over for him. A very big man. A very big, dark-skinned man. Wearing moccasins.

Samuel turned to Emma and said quietly, "Tell me everything you know about this man."

"He said to call him Nash, for Nashoba, which is "wolf" in Choctaw. I was three months pregnant when he found me walking near the Flint River, just over the Georgia line. I was considering drowning myself. He was in a wagon and stopped, looked at me for a long while, then said to get in the wagon. There was many a time afterwards that I wished I had drowned myself. We lived in a one-room cabin west of town, deep in the woods, and he beat me on a regular basis. Once Jimmy was born, I had to get out, but it took me a while to get the courage to try. On a trip to town for supplies, a woman passed close to me and whispered that if I wanted out I should go to the village. It was a while before I understood she'd seen the bruises on Jimmy and me and was trying to help."

"Emma, can you remember how to get to that cabin?"

"Well, if I remember right, you head west on that old logging trail at the end of the Harrington place. You go about a mile, and then veer off to the north about another mile. There wasn't much of a road, more like an animal track."

Samuel could see the cabin in his head. It was the cabin where he had found Mary Elizabeth.

"Did this Nash have any other cabins?"

"I don't know. He would lock me and Jimmy in the cabin and go off hunting for a couple days at a time, and I always figured he just slept in the woods. I know he had some place where he grew and stored the tobacco. And he made liquor. But I don't think it was close to the cabin. He'd be gone for a few days and come back with that sour mash smell on him."

"Have you seen hide nor hair of him in the last five years?"

"No. Thank the good Lord." Emma shuddered at the memory of what the man in question had put them through.

Samuel stood and was about to leave when Emma grabbed his arm.

"Oh, Samuel. He used to say he wished I had red hair, that he deserved a woman with red hair. My Lord, Samuel! The schoolteacher?"

Samuel nodded yes, just as Jimmy bounced back in, carrying a wrapped package. "Roxanne said to tell Miss Mae that all the supplies she asked for are in here." The boy seemed to have already forgotten his previous terror.

Samuel ruffled Jimmy's hair as he took the package from him.

"Emma, we may need to speak of this again, later. Thank you for the information."

Chapter Seven

Supper was over, and they had all drifted to the parlor, except for Charlotte. She was having a bath while Celia supervised. Celia was the twelve-year-old daughter of the newest woman in the village. Charlotte had taken a shine to her, and Mae was glad to have someone to help burn off some of that seemingly endless energy.

Mae had her sewing basket in her lap but just sat admiring her handsome husband as he thumbed through a new medical journal. Cyrus and Patrick were turning the pages of a new seed catalogue. As soon as Garth and Eleanor had gotten comfortable, Samuel stood and spoke to the gathering.

"I have some information to share with all of you."

Samuel usually sat quietly in the corner chair and worked on some small carving project in the evenings, so as soon as he spoke, all eyes turned to him.

"I believe I know who killed Mary Elizabeth."

There were several indrawn breaths. Samuel looked at Mae; he really hated telling her this, but she needed to know for her own safety.

"I found some odd cigarette butts at the cabin and at the location where I think she was grabbed. I checked with the tobacconist in town, and while he had nothing like it, he was familiar with the blend. Something made by Indians for generations, but now only known to be made in Louisiana. Anyway, Mr. Sterling ordered some in and gave me a pouch of it this afternoon." Samuel turned to Mae. "When I left his shop, I went straight to see Emma, with the pouch in my pocket. Little Jimmy is used to me hiding things in my pockets for him, so he reached in and pulled out the pouch. When the poor kid caught the aroma, he went crazy. It scared him so badly he ran screaming to his mama. By the time I caught up with him, Emma was shaking, and as white as her apron." Samuel could see the concern for her friend all over Mae's face.

"She's okay now, but you remember the man who tried to take her and Jimmy? He hasn't crossed my mind in years, but when Emma started talking, I remembered him clearly."

Edward slid closer to Mae and put his arm around her. She gave him a weak smile and laid her head on his shoulder.

"Well," she said in a shaky voice, "when you find your man, you can at least identify him by the bullet hole in his upper right arm."

"And I do appreciate you markin' him for me, sis. Now, I don't think anyone here or at the village is in any danger, but we're going to put some rules in place until this man is found. None of the women go into town alone; they need to travel in threes. And one of that three must be carrying a gun. And if there are any who have not mastered a pistol yet, I'll be driving Kathleen out this weekend to teach her, so we'll just make a class of it."

"Oh. Kathleen. Does she know yet?" Mae's voice was filled with compassion. She was aware of how badly Kathleen wanted justice for her sister's death.

"No, I haven't spoken with anyone in town yet. I'll be meeting with Captain Lance first thing in the morning to decide how to find the man. But I wanted to tell ya'll tonight so we can be on the alert from now until he's found. I'll speak with Kathleen tomorrow after school. Now, kiss Charlotte goodnight for me. I'm gonna go do a little work and get to bed early. It'll be a long day tomorrow."

Garth stood and walked out the French doors with Samuel.

"Son, I know you'll do everything you can to find this man, but you be careful. That man had a heart full of hate for us the last time he was seen, and I doubt if it's faded any over the years, if poor Mary Elizabeth is any measure."

"You're right, Pa. It would take a man full of hate to hurt a woman that bad. Tomorrow I'll start going through our old files on missing women. It's been five years since we've seen him, but that doesn't mean he hasn't been around. Thanks, Pa, but don't worry about me. You know Mama watches over me."

Garth patted his son's shoulder. "Yes, I do know. It's the only reason I sleep as well as I do. Good night, son."

Samuel spent another hour sanding the tulips he had carved into the drawer fronts of a lady's walnut writing desk. He finally laid down the fine-grit paper and dusted the surface with a soft piece of flannelette. He smiled to himself. Yep, Hansu would be proud.

****

Samuel was already at his desk when Edith Hampton arrived at work the next morning.

"Well, you're in early." She smiled tentatively.

Conversation between them seemed strained, but she was determined to patch things up.

"Mornin', Edith. What time do you expect Captain Lance in?"

"You're in luck—he's right behind me. He stopped to speak with the desk sergeant and should be here shortly."

"Thanks. If he doesn't have anything scheduled, then I need to speak with him right away."

Ten minutes later, Samuel was seated in the captain's office. It took him another ten minutes to update his superior.

"Well, son, that is a lot to take in. You're sure it's the same cabin?"

Samuel nodded. "Yes, sir, the way Emma described it, it has to be. There's not another one within a mile of the area. I have a good recollection of the man, but it would be better if I have Emma come down and let Edith do a drawing of him. I can tell you this much with certainty: he was a mean-hearted man, the kind that only gets worse with time. I checked the files on all missing women for the past five years. There are three. Four years ago, a kitchen worker at the Leon Hotel never showed up for her breakfast shift. She was twenty years old and lived with her grandfather, so it was two days before she was reported missing. No trace, no note, no known reason for her to leave. She had a boyfriend who worked with the railroad, and he had an airtight alibi. Two years ago, the oldest daughter of the Mercers—they own the feed store and gun shop on the west end of town—appeared to have left in the night. No note, but she did take a few things. They have six daughters, and the next in line said her sister had been seeing a boy from Jacksonville, so it was just assumed they had run off together. And then we come to last year. Mrs. Jenkins. Thirty-eight years old, no children, a husband who drinks heavily. She was last seen leaving church in her wagon after Wednesday prayer meeting. The general consensus was that she got tired of Wayne Jenkins's drinking and left him. Especially after he found out she had removed their life savings from the bank the Monday prior." Samuel sat back in his chair and ran his hand through his hair.

"There was a pretty extensive search done for the cook. But nothing ever turned up. The last two, well, not to slight anyone's work, but the reports show that not much was done to try to track down either of the women. And the trail is pretty cold now. But Captain, there is a thread that runs through all these women."

Captain Lance had been staring out his window during Samuel's accounting. He now turned to Samuel and waited.

"All of them had red hair."

The captain shook his head and said, "So what you're telling me is that we have a very viable suspect, but no one has laid eyes on him in five years."

Samuel nodded. "Yes, sir, that pretty much sums it up."

"All right, then, you are the lead investigator. You know what to do. Get moving, and keep me posted. As soon as you have worked up a profile and have a drawing, let me know." The captain smiled as he stood. "That's some good work, son."

"Yes, sir, thank you. I may need to spend a few days in the woods around the cabin area, sir."

"I suspected you might. Just let me know if you

Linda Tillis

need a deputy to go with you."

Captain Lance sat back down. The boy had become a man with talents, just as the captain had suspected he would. He remembered when he'd first met Samuel. He'd known from that first day that there was something deep in the young man, something that drove him to uphold right against wrong. It was an inner conviction that must be born into a man, not something you could teach at an academy. Captain Lance was grateful to have the young man on his staff and was not above using the boy's odd talents to the fullest if it would bring down a woman-killer.

Samuel spent the day assembling the known facts about the man called Nash, all the while trying not to think about what he must tell Kathleen this evening.

First, the man was vicious. He was a loner, separated from his kind. Samuel was not aware of any gathering of Choctaw in the area. Nash hunted, grew tobacco, and made liquor. And beat women and children. There were no laws against any of the three, yet. You could beat a woman and get away with it, as long as you didn't kill her, but this man had made that mistake, maybe more than once, in Samuel's territory. And he would pay for that mistake.

Nash was not a known hunter in the area, so that was a dead end. If he made moonshine, he had to sell it somewhere. That was a lead to be looked into, but for now, Samuel would stop by the Emporium and speak with Emma before he visited the schoolhouse.

****

Emma was trying hard not to let her fear overwhelm her good sense.

"I understand, Samuel. It's just that I had adjusted

62

to the idea that I would never have to concern myself with that animal again."

When Samuel started to speak, she shook her head. "I know, I know, this is the best way to find him. And I will go tomorrow and speak with the artist. I promise."

Samuel stood and placed a hand on Emma's shoulder.

"You're a lot stronger than you give yourself credit for, Emma. You've done a damn fine job of raising Jimmy. You've worked hard and learned so much since you arrived at the village. Don't let this undermine everything you've become."

Emma's eyes followed Samuel as he climbed into his motorcar. The Lord had made a special creature when he fashioned Samuel. He'd given the young man a respect and love for all women, all wrapped up in a need to protect. Someday, he would put his pure heart in some woman's hands. Emma just hoped the woman was wise enough to understand the depth of such a sacred gift.

****

Children were streaming out of the little school building when Samuel slowed the motorcar to a stop out front.

When Kathleen detected the engine over the chatter, she immediately put a hand up to smooth her wild curls. She laughed out loud at the wasted foolishness of that gesture, but she was glad she had worn one of her prettier dresses. It was a dark peach, with elbow length sleeves and a beautiful piece of cream lace at the throat.

Samuel stopped at the top stair and ran a hand through his hair. He was stalling. He reminded himself this was police business. Even so, he could not stop the tightening in his chest when Kathleen's cheeks took on a soft pink hue.

"Hello," he drawled. "Would you like a ride home?"

"That would certainly be nice," she answered softly. "Just let me gather my things."

Samuel's eyes never left her as Kathleen locked the doors and glided down the stairs. She functioned gracefully, without a lot of frivolous motion, which was unusual for such a tall woman. He caught himself watching the rhythmic sway of her hips and immediately lowered his eyes and opened the door for her. This was no time to let his mind wander.

After they were settled in the motorcar, Kathleen said, "I was planning on having pancakes for supper, if you'd care to join me. I picked up some cane syrup from the Emporium that I think your brother may have given them."

Samuel laughed. "Yep, he supplies the Emporium with cane syrup and honey, and I'd be happy to have pancakes with you."

Once they were in the kitchen, Kathleen handed Samuel a butcher knife and nodded toward the pantry. "How about slicing a couple of strips off the ham hanging in there, while I get the batter ready."

Neither of them spoke for a while. The intimacy of working together in the kitchen was pleasurable. Samuel laid the table as Kathleen pulled the platter of pancakes out of the oven and placed it in the center. When she turned to fetch the fried ham, she ran into his solid chest.

They were only inches apart.

Samuel was drawn to the flush in her cheeks. He extended a finger to brush a sprinkle of flour from her jaw. When he touched her face, her eyes closed, and she drew in a quick breath. She turned her cheek to the curve of his hand, and Samuel was lost. He lowered his mouth to hers and held her gently against his body. The kiss was long and sweet and gentle, like a soft rain in the sunshine. When he finally raised his head, a long sigh escaped her lips.

"Food," he whispered over her head. "We need food."

Kathleen laughed weakly. "Yes, I think you're right."

Samuel took her hand as they sat across from each other. He lowered his head and asked a blessing over the food they had prepared together. "Lord, bless this food, and the woman who has prepared it. Thank you, Lord, for this and all our many blessings."

"Amen." Kathleen whispered with him.

Samuel wanted to wait until later to discuss business, so they spent a pleasant half hour talking about her students and his family. Once the table was cleared and the dishes in a pan of hot water, he took her hand and led her to the settee in the parlor.

They sat together, and he put his arm around her shoulders. She looked up at him questioningly.

Samuel drawled softly, "Would you mind if I just held you in my arms for a few quiet moments?"

Kathleen turned toward him and stretched an arm across his broad chest. "I think I could stand that for a while," she whispered, laying her head on his shoulder. She was thinking she could spend the rest of her days being held by this man, when Samuel cleared his throat.

"Kathleen, I have some information for you." The softness had left his voice, and his arm tightened around her.

He was speaking in his "official" voice, and as much as she wanted to preserve this moment of peacefulness, she needed to hear him.

She sat up straighter, raised his arm from around her shoulders and gripped his hand tightly. "Go ahead."

He explained to her everything he had learned about the man who'd killed her sister.

Chapter Eight

It was a beautiful fall day, with the wildflowers putting on the last show of the year, splashing color here and there across the open fields.

To Kathleen, it seemed ironic that all this beauty should be on display for her as she rode to the manor to learn to kill.

She turned to look at Samuel as he drove. This man who evoked such joy and passion in her was going to spend the afternoon teaching her to use a gun. A long sigh escaped her.

Samuel turned toward her, and the sadness of her eyes told him she was thinking of Mary Elizabeth.

"I wish I had been able to teach her," he said softly, as he laid his hand over hers on the seat.

Kathleen inhaled sharply. How did he know? How did he know what she was thinking? She experienced a strange lightness in her mind, as if a slight breeze was echoing thru her head. She closed her eyes for a moment, and a warm peace settled over her. She imagined there was a woman whispering in her ear.

"*All will be well, dear one. You will be safe with him.*"

Kathleen opened her eyes to see that the motorcar had stopped at the village. The shouts of the children seemed to come from far away. She looked at Samuel.

"Did you have a nice nap?"

"Did I sleep?"

"Yes." Samuel grinned. "You had a nice little nap. Don't worry. All will be well."

Kathleen drew a sharp breath. "What did you say?"

Samuel stopped grinning at the sound of confusion in her voice.

"I said all would be well."

"I...thought I heard..." She broke off as her voice faded.

He touched her face gently as he repeated, "All will be well. Don't fret."

The children had been hanging clothes, and Kathleen could hear Mrs. Peters yelling over their excited squeals as she and Samuel stepped out of the motorcar.

"Do not drop those towels on the ground! Be careful. Don't trip over those baskets!" She finally recognized the futility of shouting as the children swarmed over Samuel.

After a few minutes for them to roughhouse with him, Mrs. Peters shooed them back to their chores, leaving only Celia, her mother Louise, and Kathleen to follow Samuel across the empty field to the shooting range.

Samuel was patient and took his time with the women. Kathleen and Celia were both quick to pick up on the tips he gave them for accuracy.

"Ma'am, you need to tuck that shotgun a little tighter into your shoulder. You don't want it to slip when it recoils. It could bust your chin."

Louise tightened her hold on the Browning Auto-5, and sighted down the barrel. The noise of the blast startled a flock of crows that flew away squawking their displeasure at being disturbed.

"There." Samuel smiled. "Was it as bad as you feared it would be?"

Louise laid the gun down gently on the stand Samuel had built. She rubbed her shoulder carefully. "It was louder than I reckoned it'd be, and I'm pretty sure I'm gonna be bruised tomorrow, but I think I can stand all that, if it means I can scare away some no-good varmint."

Samuel spent another three hours making sure all three women could load, unload, and clean both the shotgun and the Smith & Wesson revolver.

****

It was a beautiful Monday morning, with cool air not yet heated by the fall sunshine, and Samuel wished he could take Kathleen for a drive instead of passing out flyers to business owners.

Emma had made good on her promise to come down to headquarters and help Edith Hampton with creating a likeness of the possible suspect. The drawing was a good match. When he looked at it, Samuel could still see the angry hulk holding the arm Mae had clipped with her little beauty. Well, the man had to be getting some supplies from somewhere, and someone was bound to recognize him, so Samuel would spend the day informing business owners what to do if he was spotted.

It was early afternoon, and the air had warmed considerably, when Samuel got around to Hamish McDuff.

When Samuel entered the office, he was met by a short, barrel-chested man with ginger hair and beard. The man had on a leather apron and was shouting instructions at the top of his lungs. While waving his arms for emphasis, he caught sight of Samuel in the doorway.

Hamish had never had trouble with the law and did not intend to start now. His eyes went to the badge on Samuel's chest, and he immediately waved his worker back to the warehouse.

"Weel, good day to ye, Officer. What can I be doin' for ye this fine afternoon?"

Samuel stretched out his hand as he introduced himself. "My name is Detective Hinton, sir, and I am meeting with all the local businesses to inform everyone that we are looking for the suspect in the death of Mary Elizabeth Campbell."

Hamish nodded. "Ach, the wee little schoolteacher. 'Twas an ugly thing, that. And you say you'd be havin' a suspect?"

"Yes, sir, I have a flyer here that we would like you to show all your workers. If anyone has any information about this man, we need to know it." Samuel handed the flyer to Hamish.

Hamish took the flyer, unfolded it, and stared at it for several seconds. His heart began to pound so strongly he was sure the detective could hear it. Sweat began to gather in the small of his back.

He looked up at Samuel with a steady gaze. "Weel, I'll be passin' this on to me people, and mayhap someone can he'p ye."

"So you've never seen the man before?"

"Iffen I have, I cannot say," Hamish replied.

The average person would have found nothing amiss in his reply; however, Samuel was not the average person.

Samuel leaned against the doorframe, crossed his arms over his wide chest, and said, "I see." He continued to look at the little Scotsman.

Hamish could feel the pace of his own breath quicken, and the sweat was beginning to bead on his brow. He did not break his gaze with the tall man, even though he was afraid those gold eyes could see into his soul. He sent up a quick prayer to St. Augustine of Hippo, then turned and placed the flyer on his desk.

"I'll be sure to see that each and every one of me folks take a gander at this."

Samuel grasped the doorknob but paused for several seconds. "I would consider it a personal favor, sir. I mean to catch the man before he can harm another woman. Any help will be greatly appreciated. Good day, sir."

Hamish had seen the knuckles turn white as the big man squeezed the handle, and now he dropped heavily into his chair as the door closed behind the detective. Saints preserve us. There was no doubt in his mind that his supplier was the man the detective sought, but what to do? Turn him in? Warn him away? The man made him a lot of money, but Hamish was aware an association with the man might cost more than he was willing to pay.

The dark of the moon was still two weeks away, so he had some time to cipher out how he would handle it.

****

The woman lifted the end of the bedstead for the fifteenth time. She could tell her arms had strengthened over the last month. The cabin was small, but she paced from side to side every chance she got. She kept a length of cotton, torn from her dress, under the

71

mattress. She wrapped it around her ankle to keep the chain from chafing when she paced. She was determined to be strong enough to survive her run, for there would be no turning back. Once she broke for it, she had to make it good. He would kill her if he caught her.

He had grabbed her two nights past and fondled her breast for a moment, then placed his hand on her stomach. She had been afraid she would vomit. He knew. He knew about the baby.

She rubbed a hand over the small mound and whispered softly, "Don't worry, little one. We won't be here much longer. Mama's gonna find you a better life."

****

"So. You think McDuff may know our suspect?"

"Well, sir, he was mighty nervous about something. He didn't flinch when he studied the flyer, but he did have trouble making eye contact afterwards. Could be he's just dealin' in some shady business and doesn't want the taxman nosin' around, but he was sure uncomfortable for some reason."

Captain Lance agreed with Samuel. It would be wise to keep an eye on McDuff for a while. If Samuel believed something was off, then the captain certainly would not argue. He'd trusted the young man's instincts for several years, and he could think of no reason to doubt them now. The patrol sergeant would have someone swing by McDuff's regularly for a few weeks.

Chapter Nine

Hamish poured himself two fingers of brandy and downed it in one gulp. He would be glad to have this over and done with. He was tired of the stress of worrying over it. He'd decided on a course of action and would stick to it. When the great beastie showed up, Hamish would hand him his payment, along with the flyer, and tell him there would be no more deliveries. Surely the man would see the wisdom of making himself scarce. Tomorrow or the next night, and then it would all be over.

****

Several miles away, Nash was filling the empty earthenware jars. Tomorrow night he would deliver them to the "cinnamon man." That was his name for the man who bought the "lightning" in a jar. Nash figured he needed the money from five more deliveries. Then he was taking the woman and his son west. He would have enough saved to head to Louisiana and buy some land. He had family there, distant cousins, but Choctaw, just the same. He would be accepted because he would have a son who would grow up in the tribal family.

The sound of the wagon outside alerted the woman, and she hurried to put the bread on the table. She could never tell what mood he would be in, and could not afford to anger him at this point. Sometime in the next couple of nights he would be leaving, and she needed to be physically able to run. Few words ever passed between them, so there had been no mention of the baby. She lived in fear he might decide to rid her of it. She was aware of the scuff of his moccasins just before the door flew open. She allowed herself one quick glance to try to determine his state of mind.

No matter how hard she tried to hide it, she often shuddered at the sight of him, not that he was grotesque or anything. He was just so big and savage.

When all the food was on the table, she spoke. "I need to get water and empty the slops."

Nash pulled a rawhide cord from inside the neck of his shirt and used the key on the end to open the lock holding the chain to the iron bedstead.

The woman gathered in the eight feet of chain still attached to her ankle and balanced it across her shoulder as she picked up the slop bucket in the other hand. Once she was free from this place, she would never again use a slop bucket to pee in, she vowed to herself. She carried the bucket across the clearing and dumped the contents in the large hole she had dug. She hurried to the well and drew up a cool, clear pail of water. She poured this into the slop bucket and returned to the hole in the ground to pour out the water. It was as close to cleanliness as she could hope for, here, but soon that would change. She returned to the well and raised a bucket of water for the cabin.

When she entered, the man was finishing his meal. She was careful not to make eye contact. He had not used her body in four days, and she hoped to get through another night.

It was not to be.

Nash grabbed her wrist as she passed by, causing

her to jerk and the chain to slide off her shoulder. It landed on his foot, and he grunted in pain. With no hesitation, he backhanded the woman. She made not a sound as she crumpled to the floor.

She regained her senses sometime later, and could tell from the wetness between her legs that he had used her while she'd lain unconscious. She could make out nothing but blackness through the one high window. It was the middle of the night. No stars could be seen. She rolled to her side, with her back to the lightly snoring man. Nothing but darkness through the window. Good. He would travel tomorrow night.

****

He'd been gone about half an hour now. Her heart was pounding, and she could feel a trickle of sweat between her swollen breasts. She had to get hold of herself.

As she had often of late, she spoke aloud to the heartbeat inside her. "Okay, little one, here we go."

She had been working on the chain over a period of months. She was allowed outside when he was chopping wood, and she took the opportunity to hang clothes in the sun. She had spotted a sharp piece of granite one day and managed to slip it into her pocket. She could not work on the links nearest the ankle cuff, for fear he would catch it. So she had started on a link about midway of the eight-foot length. She was so close to having it cut through that she'd been worried it might break while he was there. She perched on one of the two chairs in the room and began to saw away with the piece of granite. She wanted to get out before it was pitch black. She would take the oil lamp with her, but the oil was low and would probably not last long.

As she worked, she reviewed everything again and again in her mind. *Don't panic. Don't thrash through the woods and leave a trail. Find the river as quickly as possible. Tie the length of chain left to your waist so it doesn't snag on anything on the bottom and drown you.* She was so intent on repeating this mantra that it actually startled her when the chain snapped.

"Oh, Lord. Oh, Lord. We're free, little one! We're free." She was suddenly weak and dizzy. She had to lower her head and breath deep to keep from passing out. Once the dizziness passed, she stood and began to gather things.

"All right, some jerky. No need to take bread; it would just get wet. The dress, the small blanket, and the oil lantern, the butcher knife, and some matches." She kept an eye on the window as she babbled to the little one. "Okay, time to go."

She stood at the now open door and looked back over her shoulder. The length of chain still attached to the iron bed frame screamed at her. *Run, run, and don't look back!* She shuddered, and her eyes filled with tears. She had lived in fear that this day might never come. She angrily swiped a hand over her eyes, pulled the door closed, and then stepped out into the deepening dusk. Lord, the night air had never smelled so sweet.

She raced across the small clearing toward a narrow trail she'd spotted one day as she hung clothes on the line. It appeared to be no larger than a small animal, but it never grew over, and she only hoped it led to the river. She could see a faint glow in the west, and the trail was running northerly, so she was pretty sure that she was headed in the right direction. She'd tied a cord through the chain and then around her waist, so she could walk freely. She held her bundle tight to her body so as not to snag on the bushes. After about twenty minutes, she stopped to light the lantern. It was now full-on dark, with the trees blocking any last light from the sun. The sound of a bullfrog chorus had been getting louder, and she finally stepped out of total darkness to see the ghostly movement of water.

She set the lantern and bundle down. "All right, little one, so far so good. Now comes the hard part. You're going to get a little chilly once I hit the water, but I'll get across as quick as an otter, I promise."

She looked out across the water as if she could see the other side. There was nothing but darkness and the soft whisper of moving water. There would not be a neat little trail on the other side of the Ochlockonee, and only heaven knew what she would have to fight on the way across. As she turned back to the lantern, she caught sight of a large, dark shape on the bank and screamed in terror. She grabbed the lantern as she scrambled backwards, expecting to be devoured by a huge gator at any moment. Her escape was stopped when her back slammed into a small tree, causing her to almost drop the lantern. She raised it over her head and stared at the shape, only to realize it was not moving. On closer look, she dropped to her knees in weakness, looked to the stars, and began to babble through her tears.

"Oh, Lord Jesus, thank you, thank you." She could hear the hysteria in her voice but couldn't seem to stop praying. "Lord, I was a-feared you had forgotten all about me. But no, you were here when I needed you most, Lord."

She scrambled to her feet and started flinging the

drying limbs off the small canoe. Yes, there was a paddle and a push pole lashed to the side. She quickly cleared the vessel and dragged it to the water's edge. She tied the lantern to a small pole at the stern but smothered the light to save the oil. She placed her bundle in the bottom of the canoe and, with one bare foot, slowly shoved away from the bank. She grabbed the push pole and started upstream.

She placed her hand on her belly. There was the tiniest of flutters, as if her partner in this escape was happy to be free. She wiped the last of the tears from her face, and as she shoved the canoe out into the black water she smiled, for the first time in years.

****

Nash lumbered along, ignoring the hard wagon seat, his thoughts dark as always. She had not opened her mouth, but he could tell the girl was pregnant. This one was his. Not like the little puling thing before. This one would be strong, and he would train him to be a man. If it was a female, he would smother it, then kill the girl. Satisfied with that plan, he imagined teaching a boy to hunt and fish.

He spent the ride calculating many things; how far along the woman was, how long he'd have to wait after the birth to head west, how much land he'd be able to afford.

It was after midnight when his wagon rolled up behind Hamish's storage building. There was no lantern hanging over the door as usual. Nash sat a moment. He did not like this. He was a creature of habit and liked things to be ordered and predictable. He climbed quietly off the wagon and approached the door slowly. As he got near, he heard the door slide on its hinges, and he froze. He could barely make out the figure of the "cinnamon" man approaching.

"Be quiet," the little man whispered.

Nash did not move. He waited until Hamish was inches away before he spoke.

"What's going on?"

"You'll need to unload in the dark. I have a candle set up inside. The taxman has been round asking questions. So be quick and be quiet."

Hamish was glad the beastie did not argue. He would give him the flyer and his pay after the wagon was unloaded.

Twenty minutes later, the big man hurried to the side of the building, where Hamish was waiting. It was time.

Hamish handed over the bag with the money. Nash took it and had turned to climb into the wagon when the little man reached out and grabbed his arm.

"Wait. There be something ye be needin' to know." Hamish held out the flyer, and when Nash took it, he lit a candle for the big man to see by.

Nash looked at the paper. It was a picture of him. He'd never learned to read. He looked at the little man. He recognized the fear in Hamish's eyes, and his animal senses took over. He grabbed the little man by the arm. Trying to keep his voice low, he said, "What the hell is this?"

Nash could see the sweat popping out on the little man's face, and his breathing had quickened.

Hamish's mouth was so dry he could barely speak. "It be a flyer the law has put out on ye. They think ye killed the wee schoolteacher."

Nash might not know how to read, but he was not a

stupid man, nor was he slow. He was holding onto the only man that might be able to place him in town the night the schoolteacher was killed. He looked down at Hamish and sensed there would be no more money from him. Ten seconds later he had removed another wad of money from Hamish's pockets and laid his broken body gently on the floor of the storage building, closing the door quietly. He was glad he had oiled that squeaking wheel as the wagon rolled away from the storehouse. He was about to move onto the main road when he realized that, even now, they might be watching for him. Without thought, he veered off to the smaller lane, just south of the main thoroughfare. As he passed the lone cottage, he wondered what the new schoolteacher looked like.

****

She was tired. It seemed like she had been rowing for hours. The muscles in her back and arms were on fire and she could feel them quivering. She wasn't sure how far from shore she was or how far she had come. She was afraid to go ashore before daylight.

"All right, little one, Mama's gonna find a tree to tie up to and rest for a couple hours. Then we'll see what we ought to do."

****

Nash could just begin to make out the forms of the trees when the wagon rolled up behind the cabin. He was so filled with rage, so needing to hurt something, that he was afraid to go inside. The woman was carrying his son, and he couldn't risk that life. Hers was of no importance to him, but a son to carry to the tribe, that was important. He unhitched the horses and allowed them to roam free. He stomped over to the well, and his anger overtook him. The damn fool woman had left the bucket on the ground. He grabbed the bucket, and in his rage he snapped the rope attaching it to the well. The cabin door slammed against the inner wall as he kicked it in. He felt around for the lantern…and found nothing.

He bellowed, "Bitch, where is the damn lantern?" He waited for the whimpering to start. They always began with the whimpering, and then the begging. Nothing. There was no sound. Not the creaking of the bed. Not her frightened breathing. He made his way to the table and lit the candle, holding it high. The candlelight reflected off the length of chain still attached to the bed frame. He hurled the oak bucket with such rage that it splintered against the far wall.

The sky had begun to lighten. A half-mile away, a herd of deer had just begun their morning graze. The sudden echoing scream of some wounded animal caused them to freeze, and then scatter toward the west.

Nash ran out of the cabin, threw back his head and filled the air with a second primal scream. He would kill her. As soon as he found her she was dead. He ran back to the well and started looking at the ground. He found her tracks leading toward the river. He ran down the trail with branches slapping his face and grabbing at his shirt. He barreled into the small open space with so much force that he toppled into the water. He rose up with a roar, slinging water in all directions. Then his eyes found the empty spot on the bank where he had left the canoe.

****

The woman woke with a start. She could see across the river. Oh, Lord, it was almost daylight. She lay there listening. Something had dragged her from sleep. Still, she could hear nothing now but the gentle lap of the southbound water slapping against the side of the canoe. She stretched her cramped body, extending her arms toward the sky. Her shoulders screamed at her. She unrolled her bundle and took out a small piece of meat. She didn't know when she might find food again, so she rolled her things back up, leaving out the butcher knife.

She had to pee. "Good morning, little one, I feel you sitting on my bladder," she whispered softly. "Just be still for a few more minutes. Mama doesn't want to pee in the boat."

She untied the boat and continued rowing north, keeping close to the eastern shore. She needed a spot clear enough to drag the canoe in and hide it. She had rowed another half hour, and her bladder was threatening to burst, when she smelled smoke. She looked at the moss and could tell the wind was coming out of the east. She must be fairly close to a camp or a house. Maybe someone who could help her find her way to Tallahassee. Another five minutes of rowing and she found an opening in the brush along the banks. She nosed the canoe in until it dragged bottom, then stepped out into the water. She tried not to break down the underbrush as she dragged it up onto the bank. She managed to drag and carry it about twenty feet into the trees before she stopped to pee.

She walked back to the water's edge, cupped up a handful and drank.

"All right, now we head inland and look for help." She rubbed her belly and then placed her bundle under one arm, with the lantern and knife in the other hand.

She had fought her way through about a hundred yards of growth when she stumbled upon a narrow path.

"Well, what do you think?" Talking to the child in her belly had become second nature now. "It's probably an animal trail, but at least it's level. All right, then, it's agreed, we'll stay on the track."

She finally stopped to lean against a tree and catch her breath. She looked up at the treetops. The wind had changed and was coming out of the north. At least, she believed it was north. The sun was up full now, and she had been trying to keep it right on her face as she walked, and besides, she couldn't smell the smoke any longer. She was about to step away from the tree when a branch snapped behind her. She froze. No. It couldn't be him. No. There was no way he could have found her. Her heart was pounding so hard she was afraid it might burst. She turned and took off down the trail like a wild deer.

She was making so much noise she couldn't tell if there was anyone behind, but she kept running. She was drenched in sweat, and her breath was becoming labored, when she suddenly burst through the trees into a large, wide field. Across the field was a small cabin with a thin trail of smoke coming from the chimney. She ran a few more feet before she heard a grunt. She looked over her shoulder, and her blood froze in her body. A bear, a large bear, was lumbering out of the trees.

The woman took off running toward the cabin again. She didn't think she had a good breath left in her, but she managed a scream that rent the morning air. She could see a small figure outside the cabin now, but her eyes were on fire from the sweat running down her face, and she couldn't tell if it was a man or woman. She had long since dropped her bundle and the lantern, but she kept a death grip on the butcher knife as she ran. Her breath was coming in short bursts of flame, and her legs had begun to quiver.

She was only fifty yards or so from the cabin when the chain loosened from her waist and fell to the ground. Her right foot came down on it, and her left ankle rolled. She was face down in the dirt before the pain could even register in her fear-fogged brain. What little air she had left in her whooshed out as her chest slammed into the ground.

Her blood was pounding so hard she could not hear, but she could feel the rhythm of the bear's gait in the ground beneath her face. She barely had time to think of dying when there was an explosion near her, followed closely by a second one, and a pained roar from the bear. A third explosion was followed by the earthshaking thud of the bear's dead weight hitting the ground.

The woman managed to raise her head and look over her shoulder. She could see the bear not thirty feet from her. She turned her head back toward the cabin and spied two bare black feet. She followed the line of those feet upward, past ankles and faded dress, and met the gaze of a wizened little woman with white wooly hair. She was holding a gun that was almost as long as she was tall.

"Lawd a-mercy! Child, you know how close you come to meetin' yo' maker?" The old woman lowered the butt of the gun to the ground and used the barrel to hold herself upright.

"That's just too much ruckus before an ole lady

done had her breakfast." She now stood over the girl on the ground. "Oh, child, yo ankle ain't lookin' none too good. You hurtin' anywhere's else? Did that animal get you? And what you doin' with a chain hooked to your leg, anyhow?"

The woman's heart had slowed to the point that she could hear over the pounding now, but she couldn't quite speak.

The old woman tried again. "Child, you gotta name? Speak up now, what's yo' name?"

The woman on the ground had curled up on her side, and now tried to sit up. The movement caused the chain to pull on her ankle, and pure fire ran up her leg. It took her a moment to recover. She stared blankly up at the old woman, as if she had no answer for her. Her mouth opened to speak but could make no sound. She tried again.

"My name is... My name is Iris. Yes, my name is Iris," she sobbed as she hugged both arms around her middle. It had been almost two years since anyone had spoken it, and she had almost forgotten her name.

Chapter Ten

Samuel woke with a start. It was the new moon, and the sky through the window was still a very dark gray. Samuel figured it was somewhere around five in the morning. He lay still, waiting for his mind to recognize what woke him. Nope, nothing came to him. Well, he was awake now, so he might as well make a start on the day.

There were no lights on in the main house yet, so he pushed his motorbike a quarter mile or so down the lane before he started the engine. He'd go on into town and check on the officers on patrol, see if any strangers had been seen around McDuff's place.

When he pulled his motorbike in front of the station, it looked like the whole nightshift patrol was gathered on the front steps.

"Mornin', Sgt. Wilkes. You boys about ready to go home and get some sleep?"

Sgt. Wilkes shook his head. "No, I don't think I'll sleep a whole lot today. Especially when Captain Lance gets through with me."

Samuel had known Howard Wilkes for several years. Wilkes had been the patrol deputy who informed them when Margaret, the housemaid, was murdered.

"What's wrong, Wilkes? Why will the captain be after you?"

"Well, it seems that while Deputy Harris was

having his supper, someone snuck into Hamish McDuff's place and killed him."

Samuel's every sense became instantly alert. "What time did you find the body?" Samuel snapped.

Sgt. Wilkes let out a long, exasperated breath. "Harris was making hourly rounds. The last time he was by there was ten thirty. He was due back at eleven thirty, but he thought he'd run home for supper first. Then he walked up on a domestic argument about midnight, and didn't make it back to McDuff's until almost two. He found the door to the storehouse open, which was not like McDuff, so he checked inside and found the man dead."

"How?" Samuel rapped out. "How was he killed?"

"His back appears to have been broken, as well as his neck. Don't worry. We have a man standing by outside the building so you can do…whatever it is you do." It was common knowledge among the force that Samuel Hinton would visit every murder scene. Not everyone understood why, but Wilkes was aware that Samuel had keen instincts about these things. Wilkes looked at Samuel now. Word had already spread that he "talked" with the dead. Wilkes wasn't one to gossip, but there was something odd about the way Samuel seemed to know things.

Samuel said, "Thanks, Sergeant, I'll head on over there now."

The sky had begun to lighten, but the man guarding the warehouse still had a lantern lit, as if holding off spirits with that yellow light. Samuel nodded to the deputy and took the lantern.

"No one has been in, sir, not since he was found."

"Thank you," Samuel said, pushing open the door.

Hamish lay in the back corner of the windowless building. His head was at an odd angle, and there was a look of surprise on his tired old face. Samuel held the lantern high and searched the floor. It was not terribly dusty, and there had been at least two people inside since the killer left. He was unable to distinguish any shoe or boot marks, or moccasins, for that matter. He squatted by Hamish and set the lantern on the floor. He spotted a sliver of something white under the body. Samuel gently rolled Hamish to his side and extracted a piece of crushed paper from under him. He turned it over and immediately recognized Edith's flyer.

"So, old man," Samuel whispered, "you tried to warn him."

Samuel gently closed Hamish's clouded green eyes. He hesitated, his palm resting on the old man's forehead.

He whispered, "Hamish, Hamish, you should have told me. What can you tell me now?"

Samuel was completely motionless, staring into the dark corner. He closed his eyes, and after a time he envisioned Nash, standing in a small clearing, his head thrown back and his mouth wide open in a scream. There was a small building with one high window. Nash stepped to the doorway, and Samuel could see the inside of the one-room cabin. There was a bed with a broken length of chain attached.

Ahh. So the big man has lost something, or someone.

Samuel stood and looked down at Hamish one last time.

"I hope you knew the Lord, old man. I hope he is welcoming you now."

****

"Well, Samuel, what do we know?" Captain Lance sat back in his chair.

"Sir, I believe Hamish tried to warn the killer. He was probably the only one in town who has seen the man in years. There were fresh wagon tracks behind the warehouse, and Hamish's foreman confirmed that there has always been a shipment of moonshine that showed up on the dark of the new moon. Hamish always took delivery himself, and no one else knows where it comes from."

The captain waited. Samuel probably had more information, but whether he would share it or not was always left up to Samuel.

After a few minutes, Samuel met the captain's stare.

"He's west of us. He has a one-room cabin in a small clearing. He's not happy. I think he's lost a captive."

Captain Lance nodded but did not speak.

After a few moments, Samuel stood and said, "I'm thinking I'll need a few days off. Might do some fishing over near the Ochlockonee."

"Going to take some buddies with you?"

"No, sir. I wouldn't want to drag anyone along. What if the fish aren't biting?"

Captain Lance stood, leaned across the desk, and shook Samuel's hand.

"You have a good trip. I expect you back in four days, whether the fish are biting or not. And if I don't hear from you by Saturday, there's going to be a search party out. Do you understand, son?"

Samuel gave his half smile. "Yes, sir, you'll have

my hide if you have to come looking for me."

The captain nodded solemnly. "Damn right!"

****

Samuel caught the children on their lunch break.

Several of them gathered around his motorbike when he stopped in front of the school, but he eventually made it to the front door, where Kathleen met him.

"Hello." She smiled tentatively. "How are you?"

Samuel motioned her back inside. "Are they all outside?"

"Why, yes, they are," she answered with a questioning look.

Samuel reached behind him and closed the door with one hand while the other arm scooped Kathleen against his chest. She raised her gaze to his and then slowly closed her eyes as his mouth cut off any questions.

The kiss was long and slow and so sweet it frightened her.

"What's going on?" she asked as he lifted his mouth from hers.

"I'm going to be out of town for a few days, and I wanted to say goodbye before I left." Samuel brushed several stray curls from her face. "I wanted to remind you to be safe, to keep the pistol with you at all times, and to miss me while I'm gone." He gave her that slow half smile, and she melted against his chest.

"Oh, I think I can manage to miss you."

Samuel let her go, but kept her hand in his. "Seriously. Where is your pistol?"

She couldn't quite meet his eyes. "I'm sorry. I left it at home this morning."

"Kathleen, you listen closely. There was a murder last night. I think it was done by the man who killed Mary Elizabeth. I'm searching for him, but I need to know that you are safe. Would you consider staying at the manor while I'm out of town?"

Kathleen paled visibly at his words.

"You are going to search for him? Who is going with you? How many deputies are you taking?"

"Slow down, now. Take a deep breath. I am going alone. I will be fine, but the one thing I don't need is to worry about you. Now, how about staying with Mae?"

Kathleen had recovered, and her eyes had taken on the steely green color. The one that meant she was digging in her heels.

"I'll be fine in my own home. I will keep the pistol with me at all times. But you, you had better take care of yourself, because I…well, I don't know what I would do if something happened to you."

Warmth settled in his midsection. It was pleasing to hear her say that. He exhaled slowly.

"All right. Just promise to be sure to lock up at night and keep the pistol by the bed. Now, I have to hit the road. So…" He gave her a hard quick kiss.

"I'll see you Saturday."

Kathleen stared after the motorbike until there was only a dust trail visible.

****

Samuel had just finished tying his bedroll when Garth stepped into the doorway.

"Mae says you're going fishing."

Samuel raised his head. His chest tightened at the sight of the worry lines visible on his pa's face.

"Yes, sir, I might spend a few days over near the

Ochlockonee. See if I can't snag a bass or two."

Garth slowly nodded. "Don't suppose you'd like some company?"

Samuel picked up the bedroll slowly, trying to choose the right words before he spoke.

"It's all right, son. I heard about Hamish McDuff. I'm guessing you need a little time to yourself, right?"

Garth didn't fully understand the workings of Samuel's mind, but it wasn't the first time the boy had gone off alone. He always returned with an answer to whatever problem he was trying to work out.

Samuel's love for Garth was reflected in his eyes as he spoke. "I'll be back soon, sir. Maybe Saturday we can fit in a game of horseshoes?"

"I think we can arrange that, son."

Garth stood, unmoving, as Samuel and Zeus faded into the distance. He hadn't said a word when his son rode off with a rifle instead of a fishing rod.

Chapter Eleven

Iris had never been so glad to see another human being. She sat in the weather-bleached wooden rocker on the porch while Granny Pearl gathered the eggs. The wizened little woman had practically carried her to the porch. She was incredibly strong for so small a person.

Iris sipped from the old tin cup of cool water she held in her still-trembling hands. Her eyes kept darting to the huge brown mound in the field. She placed one hand on her belly, hoping to reassure the little one.

"We made it. We're safe now." She was repeating this over and over when Granny's voice startled her.

"Child, who you talking to?"

Iris jumped and dropped the cup, spilling the sweet water over her feet.

"Lawd, child, you still tremblin'? Well, I'm guessin' I would be too, iffen I'd come that close to dyin'."

Iris started to babble. "I'm so sorry. So sorry I dropped the cup. So sorry…"

When Iris's voice trailed off and her eyes took on a faraway stare, Granny knew just what was needed. She walked over to the hand pump and refilled the cup, then walked back to Iris and threw the cool water in her face.

The girl jumped, spluttered, then burst into tears.

"That's right, honey, you go on and cry that scared right out. You just wail and howl 'til it's all gone. We got all day, if need be." Granny sat on a stool at Iris's side and patted her shoulder while the girl sobbed into her hands. It took a goodly while for the poor thing to let it all out. As the sobs softened to whimpers, Granny finally spoke.

"Now, honey, you need to tell ole Granny a few things. I been here on this piece o' ground for nigh onto sixty-five years. Aside from my nephew, Leon, who comes round about once a year, you the first living soul I seen since my Mason passed on, about twenty of those years ago. I know they ain't nobody just up and moved into the area, so where you come from? And what you doin' with that chain on your leg? You one of them indented folks, and you done run off?"

Between sniffling and blowing her nose on Granny's apron, it took Iris a good hour to tell her story. She finally ran out of strength and leaned back in the rocker, pale and weak, though the trembling had stopped.

"Lawd-a-mercy, child." The old woman shook her head in disbelief. "You done had you one adventurous life to be so young."

"Granny, can you get me into Tallahassee? Do you know where it is? I have to take the dress to the law and let them know where he is."

Granny had already walked across the field and recovered the pack and the lantern. She'd stopped on the way back and taken a good look at the bear and chuckled to herself. "Mason, you'd a been proud o' yor ol' lady. I hit that sucker with all three o' them shots. And a mighty good thing, or that little girl would a died for sure."

Now Granny looked at the pack lying on the porch

floor, then back at Iris. "Child, I believe it's east o' here, but I ain't left this place since Mason passed. Like I said, Leon comes round 'bout once a year and brings me bullets for the rifle, but he ain't due for three or four months. And you ain't fit to go nowhere just now. You need some food, and some sleep, and then we can talk about what we gonna do."

****

Samuel was deep in thought as Zeus made his way west. The cabin where he'd found Mary Elizabeth had been a good mile off a dirt track, and that was another mile or so off the main east/west road. The new cabin would be just as well hidden. If the killer left his place near dusk, was back home by daybreak, and was hauling a full wagon one way, he couldn't be much more than ten miles out of town. So...he'd head west and keep a sharp eye out for any wagon tracks leading off the main road.

As he rode, Kathleen filled his mind. He hoped she understood how serious he was about locking up at night and keeping the pistol close. He had no idea where the killer was, what he might be planning, or just how desperate he might be. That lack of knowledge made the man all the more dangerous.

****

Nash was sitting at the table with all his money in front of him. The second wad he'd taken from the cinnamon man's pockets had been almost two full payments, but it was still not as much as he'd hoped to have when he headed west. It was pretty near two hundred miles to Pensacola, with very little between here and there. He'd be trackin' off the main road, just in case the woman made it out of the woods alive. He needed extra bullets for his rifle if he was gonna be livin' off the land for a while. He'd make a run back into Tallahassee tomorrow night and visit Mercer's shop. He'd been in and out of there a couple of times at night, with no one being the wiser. Then he would head west. Best to travel at night for a while.

He shoved all the money into a rawhide pouch and then stretched out on the bed. He could smell the woman. The woman. He'd still love to find her and beat her to death. He was surprised she had lived as long as she had. She'd been puny when he first found her, and she'd never gotten much stronger over the years. He needed a strong woman, a large woman; one that could bear a healthy boy and take a beatin' once in a while. His mind strayed to the schoolteacher. She'd been so small as to be about useless. He hadn't actually meant to kill her, but she'd scratched his eyes. When he became lucid again, she was limp as a rag. As he drifted off to sleep, his mind held the vision of him running his hands through red hair.

****

The evening sun was low on the horizon when Samuel started looking for a place to bed down for the night. When he rode up on a small creek, he nudged Zeus off the road. He followed the creek about a hundred yards north to where it opened to a small pool.

"Well, boy, this is as good a spot as any. Let's call it a day."

By the time darkness set in, he'd hobbled Zeus, laid out his bedroll, and feasted on the supper Mae had insisted he pack. The night air was cool, but he built no fire. There was no need to let anyone know he was in the area.

****

Granny Pearl had killed a hen and made dumplin's for supper. Iris had not eaten so well since she was a child, and now she was curled up on a quilt in the corner of the kitchen. Granny sat on the back porch, drawin' on Mason's old pipe, while she contemplated what to do about the girl. It was clear she was quick with child, and it must belong to the beast that had kept her chained. Granny had rubbed a poultice on that poor ankle, but it was gonna be a while before she could put any weight on it. And how, in the name of Jehoshaphat, was they gonna get that thing off? Well, they'd worry about that tomorrow.

****

Iris woke to the smell of strong coffee. She stretched her curled body and lost her breath at the pain. Fire engulfed her left leg. She sat up and looked at it, which added fear to the fire. The foot was one large purple bruise, and the ankle was swollen so badly it nearly filled the cuff. She could only hope it would not get any larger, as that would cut off the blood to the foot. She looked up as Granny entered through the back screen door.

"Well, you finally waked up. I was afraid you was gonna sleep all day. But then, you is sleepin' for two now."

Iris was surprised. She didn't realize it was that obvious. "Well, I haven't done any serious work in the last two years, and I must have rowed that canoe at least four hours the other night. Not to mention that foot race I had with a bear."

Granny gave a big whoop. "Yeah, you was moving at a fair pace when I first spotted ya'." Then Granny caught sight of the ankle. "Lawd, chile, we better pray that ankle don't spread much more, or you gonna lose that foot! Let me help you up, and let's get it up in the air, maybe put some cool, wet compresses on it. Then we'll get you some breakfast."

****

Samuel walked down to the water's edge and filled his canteen, then led Zeus down for a long drink. While Zeus grazed nearby, Samuel ate the last of Mae's offerings, secured his bedroll, and headed out. He loved this time of day, when the birds were spreading rumors from tree to tree, the dew was like liquid silver in the spiders' webs, and the deer pranced to the open fields to wait for the sun. It was all the proof Samuel needed in order to know that the Lord had created all this for man to enjoy.

He'd been back on the road for about an hour when his attention was caught by a break in the foliage to the north. Yep, it was a wagon trail, but it was overgrown and probably hadn't been used in months. Still…he nosed Zeus to the right, and started down the trail.

****

Nash woke with a start, just as he had as a small child. He could still hear the screams from his dream. He could see his father standing over the woman, striking her again and again. The woman had stopped pleading and hung limp in his father's hands. He finally dropped her body to the ground. As his father walked away from the teepee, Nash could see the woman. She had no face, just a bloody spot surrounded by her hair. *That blood red hair.* Nash would always remember his mother as having red hair.

He shook his head, loosening the last of those

visions from his memory. He staggered to the table and held the jug with both hands as he guzzled the white spirits. Enough of the fiery liquid would drive the dreams of women with red hair from his conscious mind. Then he could sleep.

****

Samuel had gone nearly a mile. It was obvious this lane hadn't been used in quite some time, but Samuel had a feeling. He was arguing with his insides when he caught a faint whiff of smoke. Ahh…all right, he'd keep going. The lane had been angling west for some time when it suddenly opened to a large field. There was a small cabin with a thin trail of smoke from the chimney, but what caught and held his attention was in the middle of the field.

A child was trying to hook up a mule to something large. The mule was not happy and was near to dragging the poor child around in circles. As Samuel started out across the field, he kept one eye on the cabin. The mule was snorting and beginning to bray when the "child" caught sight of Samuel. She dropped the reins, grabbed a rifle up off the ground, and pointed it straight at Samuel.

"Ya'll just stop right there. What you doin' trying to sneak up on a ol' woman?" The voice was a little high, but definitely not a child.

Samuel would have laughed if that rifle hadn't been pointed right at him.

It was an old woman, and that thing on the ground appeared to be a dead bear.

"Morning, ma'am. My name is Samuel Hinton. I'm a deputy with the Leon County Sheriff's Office. Ma'am, if you could just lower that rifle, please? I'm gettin' off my horse now, real slow, so you just be careful with that gun."

Samuel slowly dismounted, then kept both hands in the air as he approached. He could see the white hair now, and the lined face that had been shielded by a large sunbonnet. The rifle was beginning to waver as those thin arms strained to hold it.

"Ma'am, I promise you, I mean you and yours no harm. I'm just in the area searching for a bad man. I've got a picture here in my pocket. If you could just take a look at it and tell me if you've seen him?"

Between holding the rifle and tilting her head so far back to look up at the man, Granny was getting a little dizzy. She had to lower the stock to the ground and lean on the barrel to get her head to stop spinning.

"All right, young fella, you just don't make any quick moves. You the first man I seen here in years, exceptin' for my nephew, so I reckon I ain't seen whoever you be lookin' for." Granny looked him up and down. He seemed clean and neat. Not like he'd been living off the land. And his horse was in good shape. Maybe he was who he said.

"Now, you tell me, you said you was a lawman? That mean if'n a body had a problem a' sorts, you supposed to help 'em, right?"

Samuel smiled. "Do you have a problem I can help you with, ma'am?"

"Well..." The old woman stopped to cackle. "I sure could use some help convincin' that mule to help drag this carcass back across into the wood-line afore those buzzards overhead start feedin'. It's gonna take 'em a few days to finish him off, an' I ain't lookin' forward to the smell. But that ain't the main problem."

Samuel waited for her to get to her main point.

She looked him up and down again. "I'll tell you what. You help with this carcass, and I'll fix you a good breakfast, and let you in on a little somethin' you might be interested in."

Samuel was in no hurry. She was an interesting soul, and she might just know something. So...

"Well, ma'am, between my horse and your mule, we ought to be able to move that carcass."

A half hour later, Samuel was pumping water for Zeus and the mule, and the buzzards had started to check out the carcass in its new location.

"Ma'am, I didn't catch your name."

"You can jest call me Granny Pearl. That's what all the young'uns call me. And can you pump that bucket over there full, and tote it in when you come inside? I'd appreciate it."

Granny entered through the back screen door while Samuel washed up at the pump and filled the tin bucket.

He took a good look around the place. Someone was obviously keeping the place up. The chicken house was in good shape, and the wire around the coop was drawn tight. No sagging to let the possums and 'coons in underneath. Granny must be near ninety years, and while she moved like a younger woman, there were just some things she couldn't have done. Like those newer boards on the roof of the barn.

Samuel took off his hat, knocked twice, and then entered through the front door. His gaze took in the inside in three seconds, and then settled on the young woman sitting at the table, her badly swollen foot resting on a chair. But, it was the cuff and chain around her ankle that held his attention.

No one spoke for several heartbeats.

Finally, Granny Pearl lifted the coffeepot she'd been holding. "You want some coffee, son, afore we get to the main problem?"

Samuel gave his almost smile and nodded. "I think that might be a good idea, Granny."

He took one of the ladderback chairs, turned the back toward the woman, and straddled it, folded his arms across the top ladder, and got comfortable.

"Good morning, miss. That's a mighty painful-lookin' foot you got there."

"My name is Iris," was all she seemed able to get out while keeping her eyes downcast.

Samuel waited. He was good at waiting.

The woman tried to sit a little straighter and grimaced with the pain. She finally met Samuel's gaze.

"Are you really a lawman?"

"Yes'm, I am a sworn deputy with the Leon County Sheriff's Office. My name is Samuel Hinton, and I'm thinkin' you have a story you'd like to tell me. Is that right?" Samuel took the cup of coffee Granny handed him and settled back to listen.

A half hour later, Iris ran out of steam. Samuel had listened carefully, but quietly, while she related how she came to be here with Granny Pearl.

Samuel stretched his long legs out, set the now empty coffee cup on the table, and reached into his pocket for the folded paper and the pouch of Perique.

"Ma'am, I'm gonna ask you a few questions now. You just answer the best you can. Is the man about my size?"

Iris nodded yes. "But bigger, you know, broader."

Samuel nodded. "All right. Does he have a scar on

his right upper arm?"

Iris's eyes opened wide as she nodded, "Yes. I always believed it looked like a bullet wound."

"Well, ma'am, you thought right. Now, did he smoke a pipe, and did it smell sorta like this?" Samuel stretched out an arm with the pouch of Perique.

The woman recoiled when the pouch got close enough for her to catch the scent.

Samuel could see the same fear on her face he had seen on Emma's.

He slowly unfolded the wrinkled flyer, and turned it around for Iris to see.

The blood quickly drained from her face, leaving her pale and shaking.

That was all the answer he needed.

He folded the paper and returned it and the pouch of tobacco to his pocket.

"Well, I'd say the first thing we have to do is get you to a doctor. That chain has to come off soon. Just so happens my brother-in-law is a doctor, and my sister is the woman you were searchin' for when you left Pensacola two years ago."

An hour later, Samuel had harnessed the mule to an old but still sturdy wagon and laid a pallet on the back for Iris to rest on. The only hard part was Granny Pearl.

"Granny, that man has already killed one woman, and I suspect him of three others. Ma'am, my mama in heaven would have my head if I left you here and somethin' happened to you. Now, let's just think of this as a big adventure. Haven't you ever wanted to see the city? I promise that as soon as we get this man, I will personally bring you home, if that's what you want. I'll put out plenty of water for the chickens, and when I come back for the man I'll run by here and check on them. Please, gather up a few things, and let me put you in the wagon."

It finally took Iris's pleading that she was afraid to go alone that moved Granny. By noontime, Samuel had the ladies loaded, Zeus tied to the back of the wagon, and was headed home.

Chapter Twelve

It was near midnight by the time Samuel stopped the wagon at the village. Iris had been asleep for a while, but moaned every time the wagon hit a bump or a hole in the road. Samuel looked over at Granny. The woman was a rock. She hadn't complained once, and her back was still ramrod straight.

The windows lit up inside Roxanne's kitchen, and as he climbed down from the wagon, a rifle barrel eased out through the front door.

"You can stop right there, mister. I got a rifle, and I know how to use it," she shouted.

"Roxanne, it's Samuel. I've got a couple of ladies who need help. You want to put that rifle down and come give me a hand?"

Roxanne had been Mae's first boarder at the village. She was now Eleanor's right hand at Taylor's, and was like a sister to Samuel.

She propped the rifle in the corner and ran out to help him with Iris. After a brief introduction and explanation, Samuel carried a groggy Iris inside and placed her in a bed. He could feel the heat from her body and was sure he needed to get Edward out here soon.

"Roxanne, I'm leaving Iris and Granny to you. I've got to get Edward."

Roxanne shooed him out. "Just go, you goose. I'll

have them settled by the time Edward gets here. And I'll have Bobby unhitch that mule and water him. Now, go!"

For once, Samuel was glad that Roxanne was so independent. She would manage fine.

Samuel considered all he had to do, as he rode Zeus across the fields to the manor. He needed to notify Captain Lance. He needed to get some deputies and some boats rounded up...but all that would have to wait 'til morning. Right now, all he really needed was a good doctor.

Ah, good. The kitchen door was still unlocked. That meant Edward might still be awake.

Samuel surprised Cyrus with a forkful of chocolate cake halfway to his mouth. Samuel laughed out loud. Cyrus's eyes were almost as wide as his mouth.

"Don't have time to talk, brother. Has Edward gone up yet?"

Cyrus lowered the fork. "He's in the library with Pa. Mae went up a couple of hours ago. What's up?"

Samuel brushed right on by his younger brother, headed to the library at a trot.

Garth and Edward were resting comfortably in front of the fireplace when Samuel burst in.

"Edward, I've just dropped off a sick girl with Roxanne. She has a badly injured foot and is running a fever." Both men jumped to their feet.

Edward said, "I'll grab my bag and meet you at the truck."

"Good. I've got to run and get a pair of bolt cutters," Samuel replied as he turned and trotted back through the kitchen.

Garth stood in the library, holding an almost empty

glass of brandy. He finally drained the glass and sat back down. He knew they would tell him what he needed to know when it was over.

As the two men sped down the road to the village, Edward said, "All right, I have to ask. What are the bolt cutters for?"

Samuel chuckled, "You wouldn't believe me if I told you. You'll just have to see."

Five minutes later, Edward stood at the foot of the bed. He shook his head in disbelief as Samuel cut the bolt holding the cuff to Iris's ankle. He wrapped the four feet of chain around his big hand, turned to Edward, and said, "She's all yours."

Edward again shook his head and said, "Check with Roxanne, and if there's not a lot of ice in the icebox, you run into town and get some."

A half hour later, Edward met Samuel in the kitchen. "Well the ice is too late for the swelling, but maybe it will excite enough blood flow to the foot to keep from losing it. Did you know the girl is pregnant?"

Samuel's head jerked up. "No. She didn't say a word. Lord a-mercy, is she going to be okay?"

"If I can get the fever to break, and she gets some rest, she should be okay. You want to tell me what's going on?"

As Samuel told him Iris's story, Edward's face got redder and redder.

"What the hell kind of beast is this guy?"

"A pretty bad one, I'd say. But I'll let you know when I get him. And I will get him," Samuel replied, as he stared at the chain coiled on the floor.

****

Samuel was up at daylight. He had the chain and

Mary Elizabeth's dress wrapped in a sheet and tucked into the saddlebag attached to his motorcycle. He'd just grab a cup of coffee from the kitchen and be off.

Mae was sitting at the kitchen table when he entered.

"Now, what are you doing up so early?" he asked.

"You try sleeping with a little angel kicking your bladder." She smiled. "And what is your excuse? Edward told me you delivered me another mother late last night."

"I've got a lot of work to get through today, so that tomorrow I can go get the killer and put everyone's mind at ease. And yes, I did furnish you with a new resident, and she's gonna need a lot of your tender love and care, Sis. She's been through her own hell on earth for the last two years. Oh, I almost forgot Granny Pearl. She's the little woman that rescued Iris from a bear. She's probably gonna fuss and say she wants to go home. You just remind her that I'll take her home as soon as it's safe." Samuel drained his cup and then patted Mae on the head as he strode out of the kitchen.

Mae's eyes filled with tears. Samuel was a pillar of strength for the community. The whole family had depended on his calm demeanor and clear head at one time or another.

He hadn't always been calm. When he was young, before Mama passed on, he'd had a terrible temper, and would fly off at the least little thing. Between Mama's prayers and Hansu's guidance, Samuel had learned to control his inner beast. But he was still her little brother, and she wanted nothing more than for him to be happy. And safe.

****

"Well. I guess the sister can tell us if it is, in fact, the schoolteacher's dress." Captain Lance raised his eyes from the dress Samuel had unwrapped. "And you say she still had that chain attached to her leg?"

Samuel nodded his head. "The other end will be attached to a metal bed frame when we find the cabin."

"All right, Detective, this is your show. How do you want to do this?"

"I think it would be best if we have a couple of men in each of two boats. The girl was very clear. If we entered the river where she left the canoe, that the only cleared spot we find, albeit a small one, on the west side of the bank, would lead us to the cabin. We can have another man on the road, in case he gets by us. He put a sack over her head the only time she was off the property, so she was unable to describe where he left the road with the wagon, so the river is our best bet. She seems to think she rowed a few miles, but it was upstream, and I figure it was closer to one mile. We can find the spot, wait until dark, and then sneak up on the cabin."

"Well, get with Sergeant Wilkes. He asked specifically to be included in the capture. He regrets that one of his men was on duty when old McDuff was killed. He'll help you line up the equipment and men that you need. Do I need to tell you to be careful?"

Samuel gave that half smile. "No, sir. I can think of three women who each tell me that at least once a day."

****

Samuel was on his way to pick Kathleen up from school. The plans had been made. Sergeant Wilkes had chosen three of his best men. The men were getting the canoes and weapons lined up this afternoon. Samuel would drive Pa's truck to headquarters tomorrow. They would load the supplies up and drive them to Granny Pearl's, and then trek out to the river.

Samuel didn't want to think about any of that now. He just wanted to spend some time with Kathleen and his family tonight.

The last of the children were coming down the steps when Samuel pulled up to the school. He climbed the steps and watched Kathleen, inside cleaning the chalkboard. He leaned against the doorframe and drank in the sight of her. While her tall frame was well proportioned, there was grace in her every gesture. Good golly, she took his breath away. He even loved the wild red hair...a shudder took over his whole body. My Lord, her red hair! She was a target for that monster.

Well, not after tomorrow. Samuel pushed off the doorframe and strode to the blackboard. Kathleen turned at the sound of his boots. Her entire face lit up when she recognized him, but before she could speak, he had wrapped his arms around her and crushed his mouth to hers.

The kiss was unlike any they had shared before, and was a little frightening. Kathleen finally turned her mouth away, and looked up at him questioningly.

When Samuel saw how red her lips were, he was ashamed. He buried his face in her neck and whispered, "I'm sorry, love. I didn't mean to be so rough. It's just that I'm so glad to see you, and you looked so darn good, and I just wanted...well, I just wanted you."

Samuel's whispers worked their way straight to her core and lit a flame that weakened her. She clung to him until she could speak. "Samuel, don't ever apologize for that." After several moments of just holding each other, she spoke again.

"I didn't expect you back until Saturday." She laughed aloud. "Not that I'm complaining, mind you. I'm thrilled you're home again. I've been so worried."

"Well, tomorrow I'll be leaving again, but only for one night. Then you won't have to worry anymore."

Kathleen arched her head back, and in a hushed voice said, "You've found him, haven't you?"

He pulled her back into his arms before he answered. "Tomorrow I will bring him in, dead or alive."

****

Samuel stared at Kathleen across the dinner table. She was deep in conversation with Mae on the merits of musical training for young children. She caught his gaze on her and turned to him. The look he gave her was enough to set her heart racing. When she turned back to speak to Mae, her face was flushed.

Mae burst out laughing.

Every head turned to the sound of Mae's laughter, and Edward asked, "What's so amusing, sweetheart?"

Mae hesitated a moment and then replied, "Oh, just your son, kicking like a mule."

Kathleen gave her a grateful smile.

Charlotte swallowed the last of her milk, wiped her mouth, and stood. "Haven't I been good, Mama? Haven't I been a good girl and didn't make a mess? Now can Kath'een play the piano for me? Huh? Can she now, Mama?"

Mae let out a long sigh. "That's Miss Kathleen to you, little missy. And yes, you've been a good girl, but Miss Kathleen may not feel like playing the piano."

Kathleen smiled. "I would be honored to play for you, Miss Charlotte."

Charlotte squealed with delight and took off running to the back parlor.

Mae shook her head and lifted her pregnant bulk from her chair. "Thank you, dear. She carried on for a week after you played for us the last time. She wanted to know how you could make the piano sound so beautiful, when it only made noise for her."

Kathleen laughed. "If she'd heard me trying to play when I was her age, she would not be quite so impressed. Mother had her hands full trying to keep me on the piano bench long enough to develop an interest in music."

"Oh, I don't have that problem with Charlotte. She loves singing, and twirling. Right now she believes if she twirls quickly her voice is louder. She nearly twirled herself through the French doors in the parlor last week. If I had her energy, I could get a lot more done each day."

When they entered the parlor, Charlotte was perched on the piano bench with a sweet, expectant smile on her little face.

"Please, Miss Kath'een, can I sit and watch, please?"

"Well, if you can be very still, I think that would be okay."

Kathleen sat gracefully and then waited until the men had taken seats.

"Charlotte, tonight I will play a very old song called 'Greensleeves.' It's about a young man and a young lady. The man loves the woman very much, but she does not love him, and he is sad."

Kathleen had played softly for several rounds of the chorus when there was a loud sniff. She glanced at Charlotte and found the child's eyes shining with unshed tears. She turned and took Charlotte in her arms. "Oh, darling, what is wrong? Why are you crying?"

The little girl whimpered. "Him's sad 'cause she don't wuv him." And she promptly burst into tears.

"Oh, Charlotte, please don't cry. He found someone else to love him, and he lived happily ever after." Kathleen turned to Edward and Mae with an apologetic smile.

Edward rose and took the crying child in his arms. "All right, missy, come with Papa, and we'll go read a story while Mama gets you dressed for bed."

Mae patted Kathleen's shoulder. "Don't fret, dear. She's been known to cry when a flower fades. She'll be right as rain once she's settled in her papa's lap. There's nowhere she'd rather be, unless it's Grandpa's lap. She is their little heartbreaker. But thank you for the music. It was truly beautiful."

Kathleen turned to a smiling Samuel. "Don't you dare laugh. I made that poor child cry!"

He put his arm around her shoulder. "As Mae told you, Charlotte will be fine. We've always joked that she had enough tears to fill the oceans twice over. She gets her sensitive heart from her mama, but she will learn, as she gets older, what is important enough for tears."

"If you say so."

"I do, and besides, I need to get you home. I have a big day tomorrow."

They were quiet in the motorcar, each thinking about tomorrow.

As Samuel brought the vehicle to a stop at Kathleen's gate, she turned and said, "Thank you."

"For…"

"For finding this beast. For finding peace for Mary Elizabeth, and for being the kind of man you are."

Samuel had no answer to that; he was the man God had made him.

Once inside, Samuel laid a small fire and then joined Kathleen on the settee.

She leaned into his chest and sighed deeply.

"Now, I won't have you worryin' about this. I'll have three good men with me, and this thing will be over before you know it."

Kathleen smiled up at him. "At least I can stop trying to remember to carry that darn pistol."

"Kathleen, it is always a good thing to be prepared. I know you're not comfortable carrying the gun, but you do know how to use it, and you never know when you might need it. Heck, you could walk up on a rattler just going to the outhouse at night. Your safety is pretty high up on my list of important things, so do you think you could try getting used to it, for my peace of mind?"

She looked into those golden eyes, and her heart spoke to her; there was nothing she would not do for this man.

"Yes, love, for your peace of mind, I will carry the gun."

****

Friday morning dawned with clouds and a chill breeze. Kathleen donned a coat and scarf for her walk to school. Once she crossed through a small piece of woods to the main road, she had the company of a few college students who did not live on the campus at

Florida Agriculture and Mechanical College. She had learned to recognize them from the blue uniforms required by the school. These young men and women were headed east, into town to attend classes, while Kathleen was headed west, to spend her day helping her little charges prepare for their higher education.

****

Samuel looked around the table as he finished his breakfast. He was meeting with his team at headquarters in the early afternoon.

Charlotte was her usual charming self, trying to cajole her papa into staying home and playing with her today.

Edward smiled as he explained, "Now, sweetheart, if you were laid up in bed with an ankle that was swollen twice its normal size, and it hurt so much that you could not walk, wouldn't you want the doctor to come and check on you?"

Samuel could see her processing this information. She was very selfish where her papa was concerned, but she was also a loving child who wanted everyone to be as happy as she was.

She finally raised a resigned face, with a smudge of jelly on the upper lip. "All right, Papa, you can go check on the hurt lady."

"Why, thank you very much, Charlotte, for being so gracious." Edward chuckled. "Now, Samuel, could you meet me by the barn? I'll just grab my bag."

Edward met Samuel, bag in hand, a few minutes later.

Samuel smiled. "You better hope this next one is a boy. I don't think Charlotte would like sharing her papa with another little beauty."

Edward shook his head. "You're probably right."

Samuel looked into Edward's eyes and froze. He immediately looked at the ground for a few seconds, and then raised his face slowly to meet Edward's stare.

"How is Mae? She feelin' okay?"

Edward had experienced this kind of thing with Samuel once before. He was not happy to see that odd look in Samuel's eyes; as if he already knew the answer to the question he asked. Edward stood a little straighter. "Samuel, is there something you'd like to share with me?"

Samuel just looked at him. This man loved his sister more than life itself, and there was nothing he would not do to insure her safety and happiness; he'd proven that five years ago. Edward had learned the hard way that we are not always in control of our lives, or our happiness; that the good Lord has a plan for each of us, and that sometimes we just have to leave things in His hands.

Samuel turned to stare out across the fields. "How far along is Mae now? When do you think the babies are due?"

Edward opened his mouth to answer, then froze. His mind had just processed what his ears had heard. "Did you say 'babies'? Why did you say 'babies'? Samuel, answer me!"

Samuel turned back to the man he had come to trust and love. "You tell me. Could there be more than one? Wouldn't you be able to tell by now?"

Edward paled and slowly lowered himself to a bale of hay. Mae had gotten larger much sooner this time. She often seemed drained of energy, and they both attributed it to chasing after Charlotte. Good grief, what kind of doctor was he, that he could miss something like this? In his own wife?

Edward stood slowly. He looked at Samuel, and he wasn't sure what to say. He had questions, but he wasn't sure he wanted to know the things Samuel seemed privy to.

He finally spoke. "I think I'll just go back inside now. Maybe give Mae a checkup."

Samuel patted Edward's shoulder. "You're a good man and a great doctor, Edward. And you know whose guidance to seek if you need help. All will be well."

Samuel observed a slight wobble in Edward's stride, as he headed toward the kitchen door. Samuel grinned to himself. *Two little boys to teach to fish. Boy-howdy, Garth Hinton is going to be one happy grandpa!*

****

Sergeant Wilkes had checked the rifles himself. The canoes, paddles, and push poles were all in good shape. Of the three men he'd handpicked for this mission, two were strapping, farm-raised boys, so the rowing would be easy. The third man would take the truck back out to the main road and head west. He would take up a position about a mile west of the bridge over the Ochlockconee. His job was to watch the road.

When Samuel arrived with the truck, Sergeant Wilkes and his men were glad to get started. Once loaded, the three deputies jumped in the back, while Sgt. Wilkes slid into the front with Samuel.

"I'll be glad when this day is over. A lot of women will sleep easier tomorrow night."

Samuel turned to Wilkes. "You do know that Hamish caused his own death by trying to alert the

117

killer, right? There was probably nothing you or your deputy could have done to help him once he made that choice. Except maybe have died with him."

Wilkes nodded. "I know that. The old man was a fool not to realize the danger he put himself in, but that was no way for an old man to die."

The truck left the main road around four in the afternoon. By five, the four men had unloaded the truck and started the trek to the river, while Deputy Harris headed west on the main road.

Samuel noted there was not much left of the bear carcass as they passed it. The others were impressed with the size of the skeletal remains. "You'd be even more impressed if you'd seen the size of the little old lady that took him down." Samuel laughed. "I swear she's not more than four and a half foot tall, and couldn't weigh much more than eighty pounds, but when she held that rifle on me, I was sure she was all business."

The men followed the bear tracks till they located the cut-off Iris had taken. The girl had made no attempt to cover her tracks after she left the river, so the men had no problem finding where she had dropped her canoe. It was now coming on to dusk, so they launched the canoes and started the ride south.

Samuel had reckoned Iris probably overestimated the distance she had rowed that night, rowing upstream, in the dark, and scared to death.

"You fellas know how sound travels on water, so let's keep the chatter down and find the opening in the brush, as much before dark as possible. Then we'll give it an hour or so before we close in." And with that, Samuel picked up his oar and started paddling.

****

Nash took another look around the cabin. He wasn't taking the wagon, since he'd be off-track most of the way. He'd rolled the blankets around the few items he'd be taking and tied them to the saddle on the spare horse. The sun had dropped below the tree line in the west. He figured to get to Mercers' around eleven. He knew from previous experience the old man had his brood in bed by nine every night. They lived in a large cabin a couple hundred feet into the woods behind the business. His mind wandered to the night he'd taken the girl. It was the second time he had come in the night to get ammunition. She'd been in the outhouse out back. He'd seen the light from her lantern through the cracks. He would have waited until she'd returned to her bed, but when she stepped out of the toilet she'd raised the lantern to light her way. The light had reflected off the long curls falling nearly to her waist. The dark copper seemed alive, as her hair swayed above her hips. Two long, silent strides, a huge hand over her mouth from behind, and he caught the lantern with his free hand as she dropped it to struggle. He had used her for two days before she started bleeding. Then he'd taken her down to the river, carried her body a few miles past the bridge, and dumped her into the river for the gators.

****

Samuel held up a hand. The deputy in the back of the canoe immediately stopped rowing and slowed the boat, as did the two in the canoe trailing them. He had spotted a break in the brush at the water's edge ahead. The deputy quietly laid down his oar and took up the pole. He nosed the canoe over to the opening and held it there just off shore.

All four of them could just make out the small cleared area and see how it narrowed to a trail about fifteen feet in. The last of the day's light was fading fast, and that was okay with Samuel. They rowed back up the river about fifty feet and tied up to some low-hanging branches.

"We'll just wait here for another hour, and then ease on in." Samuel could barely see three heads nod in the gathering darkness.

Chapter Thirteen

Kathleen's mind strayed again from the papers she was grading. It was almost dark. Samuel and his men would be somewhere on the river now. He had explained his plan to her twice. He was just trying to reassure her, but it was a wasted effort. She would not sleep a wink until she knew he was safe. Her stomach growled, and she remembered she had not yet eaten. She would go to the kitchen and find something to nibble on. Maybe that would settle her nerves some.

****

Nash reached the main road and steered his horse around the lattice frame blocking the wagon track. This time of year it blended well with its surroundings; a few dead limbs woven through gave it the appearance of a brush pile. Not perfect, but enough to keep the average person from investigating the worn ruts behind it. He looked westward. The sun had dropped behind the tree line, and the light was fading quickly. Even so, he wasted no time crossing the main road and moving south into the woods. He'd stay in the cover of the woods until he neared town. No point in taking chances.

About a mile east, and around a slight curve in the road, a bored Harris leaned against the truck fender, staring off into the west. The lime rock covering the roadbed made it visible for about a hundred yards, while all else faded into the oncoming darkness. He waited patiently for the two gunshots that would tell him the others had made the capture. The shots would also tell him the general direction of the cabin.

He never saw the two horses cross the road and disappear quietly into the woods southwest of him.

****

Samuel released the rope from the branch that had kept them stationary for the last hour and a half. Both canoes drifted back out into the southbound flow of the Ochlockonee. No one spoke as both canoes were edged into the opening along the west bank. The canoes were pulled silently from the river and placed side by side on the ground. The men formed a single line, with Samuel in the lead.

Samuel took his time, taking care not to rattle the underbrush. His mind played a vision of Iris running along this path, unable to see but too frightened to be cautious. The girl had grit, that was for sure.

After half an hour, Samuel sensed, more than saw, a widening to his left. He stopped and listened for several seconds. He could make out the shadow of the cabin across a small clearing.

He was gone. Nash was gone. Samuel could sense no life force beyond his and the three men standing motionless behind him. Still, they crept cautiously across the clearing toward the cabin. When they approached the northeast corner, Samuel spoke one word softly.

"Light."

The deputy at the rear lit the oil lantern he had been carrying, and passed it up to Samuel. Samuel held it high, and they could all see the well on their left.

Samuel stepped to the open door of the cabin. He walked in and held the lantern high.

The men behind him could see the shattered oaken bucket at the base of the far wall. There were indrawn breaths when their eyes landed on the length of chain still attached to the iron bedstead.

Samuel's attention was held not by the chain but by the absence of blankets on the bed. Nash was gone. He had taken his meager belongings and left.

Samuel turned to the others. "Well, we've missed him. We may as well follow the wagon tracks out to the road and locate Harris and the truck. We can come back for the boats later."

It took them almost an hour to find the lattice frame covered in vines and limbs. Once around the frame, Samuel gave orders.

"Bob, you head west, with the lantern, and we'll head east. Whoever locates the truck first will come and find the others. When we get back to town, we'll round up some dogs and come back and get a direction on him."

The three men with him could hear the frustration in Samuel's voice.

****

Nash heard the screech of an owl. He stopped his horse and waited. He strained to hear the answering screech. The forest was silent. This was not a good sign. From somewhere in his early memories there was mention of a lone owl. He remembered sitting at the knee of an old woman as she told the young ones the history and legends of his people. The old woman's face had reminded him of a dried apple, all brown and shriveled. She had told them if you heard the *ishkitini,* the horned owl, call in the night, you should listen for the answering call. If no second call came, then you would know it was the *shilombish*, your death spirit warning you.

Nash shook his head; this was foolishness from an old woman whose tales had long since been forgotten. His mind knew this, but his *shilup*, inner spirit, told him to be vigilant as he neared the edge of town. He would get what he needed from Mercer's place and head back west quickly. No need to test his luck. He was confident that the bitch was still lost in the woods, or at the bottom of the river; however, he continued to listen for the responding screech.

****

Kathleen unfastened the brooch from her blouse and looked at the little watch face inside. It was almost one o'clock in the morning. Surely by now Samuel had captured the killer. Hopefully he would come soon to tell her all was well; only then would she be able to sleep. She shivered, not with fear but from the cool of the night. Oh, shoot! She'd forgotten to bring in wood, had not laid an evening fire, and the temperature had dropped drastically since sundown. Now she would have to make a trip to the woodpile.

Kathleen was over half way to the pile of logs, stacked neatly at the far edge of the picket fence, when she remembered the pistol. She shook her head. Just how was she to carry a lantern, logs, and a gun? Samuel need never know. Kathleen propped the lantern along the upper edge of the fence and bent to pick up a piece of wood. As she lifted the rich smelling pine to lay it across her arm, she saw a large spider crawling up her arm. With no care for the consequences, she threw both arms in the air and screamed like a banshee.

****

The men had traveled less than a mile when they located Harris; a quick two miles west to pick up Bob and they were on their way to town.

As the truck headed east, Samuel silently berated himself. He should have come back the same night he'd given Iris over to Edward's capable hands. He should have at least returned the very next day. As his anger with himself grew, he remembered Hansu.

After the death of his mother, Samuel had been angry with the whole world. At least once a day he would experience a need to break something, a need to feel he had control over something, even if it was only the choice of what to break.

Hansu had seen the boy's tightly held pain. The wise old Chinese man had already begun training the boy in the martial arts, so he had stepped up the pace. When Samuel would lose his temper, the old man would push the boy until the anger drained. He would make the boy run, sometimes for miles, taunting him the whole time. Samuel could hear him: "What matter, boy, you no can keep up with old man? You not as fast as you think you be?"

Some days there would be piles of broken boards littering the clearing behind the cabin. Eventually, Samuel learned to channel his anger into pure energy. Those would be the days that he outworked most of the men at his father's sawmill. As he grew, physically and emotionally, there was less and less anger, and Samuel settled into the quiet, seemingly passive young man he presented to the world.

Samuel laughed inwardly as he drove. If the old

man were here now, he would say, "Sammy, you need cool head; you need slow down and think."

Samuel turned to Sergeant Wilkes. "Howard, who has the best bloodhound in the county?"

"I was just thinking about that," Wilkes replied. "I'd have to say my cousin Lester. His ol' Albert has been known to track for three days. Lester lives on the east side of the county, near Mallard Farm. I could drop you at your place, take the truck and run over to pick up Albert, and be back to you in an hour."

"Good. That'll give me time to saddle up Zeus, grab us some food, and meet you back out at the main road."

****

Nash was westbound again. As he took a long draw on the whiskey bottle, he thought of the several boxes of ammo tucked in his saddlebags. It would make no difference now if they were found to be stolen. He would be long gone by daylight. He was deep in his plans when a scream rent the night air. His horse reared, and he was nearly thrown. While the scream still echoed in his head, there was an explosion of light followed by flames.

Even as his mind told him it was not his *shilombish,* he saw the fence around the lone cottage ahead of him was on fire. He moved forward cautiously, leading the horses to the north side of the lane. As he neared the fence, what stood out behind the flames caused his heart to jump in his chest. He swiped a large hand over his face, and blinked in disbelief. A woman stood framed between the fire and the light from the cottage. Nash could see that she was tall. And that her red hair seemed to dance in the light of the fire.

Kathleen stood frozen as the oil from her shattered lantern took flight in flame and spread along the old, dry fence. She needed to do something. She had to make sure the fire did not reach the cottage. Water! Her brain finally broke through her shock from the spider. Water!

Kathleen turned to run into the cottage for a bucket of water, but froze in mid-turn. Her eyes had found Nash in the darkness. She had seen the flyer. Standing in the dancing light of the burning fence, he was even larger than she would have imagined. And more frightening. She took two steps backward. Her mind was locked. She could not make it past him to get inside. Inside, where her pistol lay atop the dresser.

She took another two steps backward. Neither of them spoke, and the only sound was the crackling of the blaze as it devoured the fence. So she was even more startled when he shouted, "No! Don't move!"

He started running toward her, and at the same moment, she felt the heat. She had backed into the flames and set her skirt on fire.

When he grabbed her, she fought like a wild animal, one who sensed death was near.

Nash struggled with the woman, trying to get his hands on her smoldering skirt. He finally did what needed to be done. A right clip to her jaw and she crumpled to the ground. He rolled her over a couple of times, then ripped away the smoking outer skirt from her body and threw it aside.

Nash now stood over the unconscious woman. Lying there, with her white blouse and white petticoat, she looked like a white dove…the dove that the Great One had turned into a wife for the lone survivor of the great flood. In Nash's whiskey-fogged mind, she was a gift. This was the woman who would give him strong sons. Nash finally noticed the fire was spreading down the fence and into the yard. He lifted the woman from the ground as if she were a child. He cradled her close to his chest as he carried her to the horses.

****

Samuel was entering the circular drive in front of the manor when the vision danced before his eyes. He slammed on the brakes, throwing the deputies in the back to the floor of the truck bed. He had jumped from the truck and was reaching for the rifle behind the seat, by the time Sergeant Wilkes could draw breath.

Wilkes had just opened his mouth when Samuel shouted, "I can't wait on the dog. I'm grabbing my horse. You go get the dog and start at the schoolteacher's cottage. I'll try to leave you a trail."

Samuel could hear the truck speeding off as he raced toward the barn. As he passed the kitchen, a light came on. He did not have time to explain, so he kept running.

As he tightened the cinch, Garth spoke from the barn door.

"Son, are you leaving again?"

Garth held the lantern high, and when Samuel turned, his face reflected the fear he was trying to hold at bay.

"What is it, son? What's happened? Are you hurt?"

"Pa, he has Kathleen. Can you saddle the roan while I grab a canteen of water?"

"Who, son, who… Oh, dear Lord, not your killer?" Even as he asked, Garth was grabbing the saddle and heading for the corral.

Samuel was already halfway to the house, and by the time he got back, Garth had the roan saddled, with a lead rope secured to the pommel.

Samuel grabbed the rope from Garth's hands and then paused to face him. "Pa, I need you to pray. Pray that Kathleen is alive. Then pray for me, Pa, 'cause I intend to kill the man, in either case."

Garth's heart filled with pain as he said, "Son, you bring that girl home, and you do what you need to do to make this right."

Samuel nodded, hung the canteen from his saddle, shoved into his saddlebag a towel full of biscuits he'd grabbed from the pantry, mounted Zeus, and rode off into the darkness.

****

Kathleen was dreaming. She dreamed she was lying face down in a boat that swayed gently, from side to side. In her dream she knew she needed to wake up, but she couldn't quite open her eyes. Her mind kept saying something about water. She needed to get water. But the boat was in water, so why did she need more? She became agitated with herself. She needed to get water. Suddenly there was a soothing voice in her ear. *Samuel is coming. Stay calm, and all will be well.*

Kathleen opened her eyes to darkness. Darkness and pain. The left side of her head throbbed, and her arms were extended and tied around a horse's neck. She half lay atop a horse. One moment she was confused and uncertain, and in the next she was about to scream in terror, as realization of her circumstances wiped the fog from her brain. Before she could scream, the voice whispered again.

Sshh, no screaming. Stay calm.

Kathleen froze. That voice was familiar, maybe from a dream? But this was no dream; this was a nightmare. Where was Samuel? How did this man find her, and where was he taking her?

She tried to sit up in the saddle, and her movement caught his attention. The horses stopped, and the man turned in his saddle to look at her. When she saw the look on his face, she realized the night around her was not as dark as she first imagined. In fact, the pre-dawn gray told her they must have been riding for at least three or four hours. The longer he looked at her, the faster her heart raced. She opened her mouth to yell at him, but the *Ssh* in her ear stopped her. She sat as straight as she could, considering the way her arms were tied around the horse's neck. After a few moments of them exchanging stares, the man directed his horse to her side.

It was all Kathleen could do to hold in a scream, as he reached out and untied the rope holding her arms around the horse. After another long look, he grunted, nodding as if he approved of her silence.

He wound the rope around both wrists, then around the pommel. He stared at Kathleen for several moments and then started forward again, still holding the tether between the two horses.

Kathleen's head throbbed. She was grateful he had untied her arms, as her right arm seemed stiff in the elbow joint. She would have loved to rub some circulation back into her arms, but that was not to be.

Chapter Fourteen

Samuel made it to the cottage just before daylight. The burned fence made a neat line of ash alongside the road. It appeared that a south wind had edged the flames back on themselves and kept them away from the cottage. His heart tightened in his chest at the sight of Kathleen's partially burned skirt lying on the ground.

A quick look inside revealed her pistol lying on the dresser. Sometime in the future they would discuss the importance of her listening to him, but right now all he could think of was the fear she must be feeling. Oh, she was still alive. His heart would have told him if she were not.

Samuel grabbed a blanket from the bed. He rolled it up and shoved it into the saddlebag the roan was carrying, then climbed back on his horse and paused to think. Obviously, the man was headed west. He was no fool and would be staying off the roads. He would probably be south of the rail line. Samuel looked at the sky. It was now daylight, but the sun was obscured by clouds. The same south wind that had saved the cottage would probably blow in rain this afternoon. Samuel made a decision. He estimated the man had four to five hours' head start on him. He would head west along the rail line for the first few hours, then angle southwest, hoping to make up lost time.

****

Kathleen kept silent as long as possible. The sun was about a quarter of the way up in the sky. She didn't want to draw the man's attention, but she had no intention of peeing in her drawers. She finally worked up her nerve.

"Excuse me." Her voice sounded weak, even to her ears.

The man gave no indication he had heard.

"Excuse me," she tried again.

He never turned or slowed.

"I have to pee!" Kathleen shouted. Her horse did not like shouting. She would have been thrown if not for her death grip on the pommel. When the horse had calmed, the man spoke.

"Do not yell. If you do, I will shove something in your mouth. Do you understand me?"

His voice sounded from deep in that barrel chest, but his words sounded short and choppy, as if they were rarely used.

"All right," she replied. "I won't shout again, but I must get off this horse for a moment."

He dismounted and walked to her side. He was so tall his shoulders were higher than the horse's back. He loosened her wrists from the pommel but left them tied. He reached up and grabbed Kathleen around the waist and roughly jerked her from the horse. When her feet hit the ground, she found her legs too weak to hold her, and she began to slump. The man grabbed both her arms to steady her, and she had to bite her lip to hold back a scream.

"My arm," she whimpered. "Let go of my arm." She leaned against the horse as she held up her wrists and looked at her right arm. There was a large red swelling that was obviously tender to the touch. The spider. Oh, good heavens, the spider must have bitten her. She almost laughed aloud, as her eyes filled with tears. Here she was, being hauled to God only knew where, behind a known murderer, with no help in sight. Yes, the spider bite was the least of her worries.

The man released her arm even though he was not moved by the tears in her eyes. "What bit you?"

"It must have been the spider. It crawled out of the firewood. That's what made me drop the lantern."

He just stood there, as if waiting for more.

"The lantern burst against the fence and started the fire," she snapped.

He took her wrist in one hand and turned her arm to better see the bite.

He looked at her face. She was pale. When he raised a hand to feel her face, she whimpered and flinched. His hand stopped in midair. For some reason, he did not like her flinching. He did not want this woman to fear him. It made him angry. He had done nothing to cause her fear. Hell, he had saved her from being burned alive.

He touched his hand to her forehand. Yes, she had a fever.

"You are sick from the spider bite. The poison has been in you many hours, and I cannot get it out now. You will be more sick by dark." He looked at the gathering clouds in the southwest. "Rain will come later and cool your fever. Now, pee."

Kathleen raised a hand to her face. Yes, she was warm, and she did not feel well. She had attributed her nausea to fear. She stepped away from the horse and walked behind a large oak. She was grateful he did not follow her. And she was grateful she had been wearing her only pair of split drawers under her now singed petticoat. She was able to stoop and relieve herself. As she started to stand, her eye caught sight of the ragged, burned edge of the petticoat. She quickly tore a small piece off and laid it at the base of the tree. Maybe, just maybe, someone would find it, and her.

As she approached the horse again, she made a decision. She had no idea where she was, and if she tried to run from him she might die in the swamps; however, if she found an opportunity to kill him, she would take it.

Nash tossed her up into the saddle, then handed her a canteen.

"Drink to cool your fever. We will eat tonight."

Kathleen took in long swallows of water, then returned the canteen.

He re-tied her wrists to the pommel, climbed back on his horse, and headed southwest. He made plans as he rode.

This was the woman he was meant to have. She would be the one to give him strong sons. He would not touch the woman until he could present her before the tribal council. This was right. He was sure in his heart that this was the problem with the others. He had taken them without the approval of his brothers, and they had proven their unworthiness by angering him. They had forced him to kill them.

He remembered seeing, as a child, the council convene over the pairing of a couple. Yes, this time he would do right. If this woman wanted to live, she would be wise. She would not anger him. He was pleased. He reached for the jug secured to his saddle and drank long from the white spirits he himself had made.

****

Samuel looked at the sky. There was definitely a storm building. It was past noon, but there would be no stopping to eat. He had refreshed his canteen at a creek a mile or so back. He briefly considered Sergeant Wilkes and the bloodhound. It didn't matter how far behind him they were. The outcome of this rested on his shoulders alone. Well, his and the Lord's.

For the last half hour he'd been remembering some of his mama's favorite Bible passages. Passages like Mark 11:25, which said, "And when you stand praying, if you hold anything against anyone, forgive them, so that your Father in heaven may forgive your sins."

Samuel would have to rely heavily on the Lord's grace and forgiveness, because it was clear to him this man would never face the judgment of his peers. No, he would have to kill him, either to get Kathleen back or because he was too late to save her. There was no forgiveness in his heart for Nash. For whatever perverted reason, the man had become a stone-cold killer of women. Stone-cold. Ah, Samuel remembered another verse, Romans 13:4, saying, "For he is God's servant for your good. But if you do wrong, be afraid, for he does not bear the sword in vain. For he is the servant of God, an avenger who carries out God's wrath on the wrongdoer."

Samuel had never considered himself an avenger, but he did believe the laws of man had to be obeyed. Some men were born to uphold what is right and good in this world. Samuel reckoned that was the duty God had placed in his heart when he was born. A duty to uphold justice. That was what he'd sworn to do when he took this job, and that was what he would do when he found Nash.

Samuel had never tried to "call" his mama before. He didn't know if that was even possible. But just in case, he spoke aloud. "Mama, I know you watch over me, but you need to leave me on my own now. I need you to watch over Kathleen and keep her safe. She's my heart's destiny, Mama, and I know she'll be okay with you protecting her."

****

Kathleen was having trouble staying awake. She was unable to piece two coherent thoughts together. The big roiling clouds she had seen earlier had blocked out the sun, and she could hear thunder in the distance. She should probably close the windows, in case the wind started blowing. And she had clothes on the line out back, and if she didn't hurry they would all get wet. When her head fell forward, she instinctively jerked upward and opened her eyes.

Her mind cleared for a moment. Dear Lord, she could see the man on the horse in front of her. She wasn't home. She didn't even know if she still had a home. Maybe the little cottage had burned, along with the fence. She wanted to feel her face to see how hot she was, but her hands were still tied. Her clothes were like lead weights against her body, and her eyes seemed to be bulging from pressure within. She was consumed by a sudden weakness, just before she lost consciousness.

There was a whimper, and Nash turned in time to see the woman falling forward. He jumped from his horse and ran to catch her as she slid off her saddle. He could feel the heat from her body before his hands ever touched her. Damn. She was burning up.

He quickly untied her from the pommel and lowered her to the ground, looking up at the sky as a streak of lightning sizzled its way to the ground. The following boom of thunder scared the riderless horses into panic, and he was barely able to grab the tether rope in time to prevent their escape. He had to leave the woman on the ground while he secured the horses to a medium-sized scrub oak.

As the rain started falling in big fat drops, the kind that stung when they hit, he grabbed a bedroll from his horse and was halfway back to the woman when the hail started. He hoisted her over his shoulder and quickly surveyed the area. When he found a large fallen log, he laid the woman on the ground alongside it, cut a stout limb from a nearby pine tree, and using that as a tent pole, threw the blanket from the bedroll over the limb. Holding the pole as he sat on the fallen log, he extended his legs over the unconscious woman. She had been soaked through by the time he had the shelter over her.

Well, she needed cooling. He looked down at her. Her right arm was swollen half again its normal size, and an angry red extended two inches above and below the elbow. He was going to have to make a poultice for that arm. He reached for his tobacco pouch. He took a wad and placed it in his mouth. He chewed until it was softened, then placed the wad over the center of the bite. He cut a strip from the bottom of her petticoat and wound it around her arm, securing the wad of tobacco to the wound.

By the time he had finished dressing the wound, the hail had stopped, and the rain was down to a slow but steady shower. He looked at the woman. *Well, she can't stay in the saddle unconscious, so I might as well rest now.* He lay down on the ground with his back to the woman, threw the blanket loosely over their heads, and within minutes was asleep.

Chapter Fifteen

Samuel took his shirt off and wrung the rain from it. The moon slipped in and out of the now empty clouds, allowing the occasional sight of the creek, swollen from the earlier, raging storm. Samuel had stopped to let Zeus drink and allow himself a moment to stretch his legs. He had turned southwest an hour before the sun dropped below the tree line.

The CT&G Railroad Company had settled a small town in Wakulla County. If Nash wanted any supplies, that would probably be his last chance. Samuel expected him to stay away from the coastline, to avoid the many fishing villages. Sopchoppy was about as far south as he would risk. So…Sopchoppy was where Samuel would head. Once he hit the rail line, he would just follow it on into town.

Samuel stretched his arms over his head and tried to ease the tension in his shoulders. He was tired, but there would be no stopping. He needed to get to Sopchoppy ahead of Nash and alert the storekeepers.

Samuel knelt by the creek and refilled his canteen, capped it, and then bowed his head. He spoke his prayers out loud as if he spoke not to the King of Kings but to a trusted friend and advisor.

"Lord, you know my needs. You know what's in my heart, and what I plan to do when I find this man. I ask your forgiveness now; forgiveness and the strength to do what has to be done to save others. I thank you, Lord, for bringing me Kathleen. And if this doesn't end in a good way, Lord, at least I've known the love of a good woman. In the name of your Son I pray, Amen."

****

Kathleen became aware of her surroundings slowly. Her damp blouse and petticoat clung to her aching body. Something was hovering above her face. She could feel a rising panic. Her heart began racing, and she opened her mouth to scream. She was stopped by the *Sshh* in her ear. She jerked to a sitting position, which slammed her face into the cold, wet blanket. She began to fight the blanket, swinging her arms wildly and whimpering as she fought.

Suddenly the blanket was gone, and she could just make out the hulking outline of the man. All the fight whooshed out of her in one long exhale as her memory returned. She was being kidnapped. By a murderer. The man who had killed her sister.

"Be still," he commanded, as he wadded up the blanket and threw it aside.

Kathleen's mouth was as dry as cotton. "Water, please," she whispered.

As she drank from the canteen he handed her, she didn't think water had ever tasted so good. She lowered the canteen and noticed she was wet. All over.

"Why am I wet?"

He reached out and touched her face. It was cool to the touch.

"Rain," he answered. "The rain has cooled your fever. How does your arm feel?"

When Kathleen extended her right arm, she saw the bandage around the elbow. Her every muscle was sore from the hours of riding and lying atop a horse, so it was hard to tell if the spider bite was still paining.

"All right, I suppose," she answered cautiously. She was unsure how to interact with the man. She was sure he would kill her, with no hesitation, if she gave him a reason. And then there was the "voice" that kept telling her to be quiet. Maybe that was the fever. Of course. It had to be the fever. She must have been delirious.

"Here, eat this."

Kathleen looked at his outstretched hand. She had no idea what he was holding but was sure she didn't want it.

She was about to tell him what he could do with it when the voice said, *It's all right. It's just jerky. Suck on it until it softens.*

Kathleen jerked her head from side to side, searching for the owner of the voice. There was no one there. She was alone with the man. She must be losing her mind. Yes, that was it. Twenty-four hours and already she was crazy.

The man could see Kathleen's confused face, as she turned from side to side, as if looking for someone. Just then, softly, as if from far away, sounded the call of an owl. The man froze, waiting for the answering call. But none came. The big man shivered, as if from the cool night air.

The moon broke free of the thin wisps of leftover clouds, and Kathleen could see his face. No, it was not the night air. The big man was frightened.

****

Howard Wilkes was tired. He was wet and tired. And worried. What if the rain washed away the trail?

But then, Ol' Albert just kept dragging him along, so they must be on the right track. He'd never known Albert to fail. They'd probably been four hours behind Samuel Hinton when they got to the cottage. Samuel was on horseback so there was no danger of overtaking him. They'd found the partially burned skirt lying in the yard. It took Albert about three whole minutes, running around the area, to pick up the scent. That had been a day and a half and one hellacious storm ago.

Howard had seen the wild look in Samuel's eyes when he'd jumped out of the truck.

"Ya know, Albert, if I was a bettin' man, I'd say that boy was in love with the schoolteacher."

Albert turned to look at the deputy, threw back his head and howled in agreement, then started urging the deputy in a southwesterly direction.

****

Samuel was headed west. He'd hit the rail line about an hour ago and figured he couldn't be more than five to ten miles from Sopchoppy. He'd eaten the last of the biscuits he'd snagged from the pantry. By his calculations, it was about two in the afternoon. He hoped to make it before nightfall. He didn't think Nash would come into town until the stores opened in the morning.

A long four hours later, the sun dropped below the horizon. Samuel rounded a large bend in the tracks and saw light ahead. He looked up at the evening star that was just beginning to twinkle.

"Thank you, Lord. Me and Zeus are about worn out."

Zeus raised his head and whinnied.

Samuel looked around as he rode into town. He

passed a small station office that was closed. He pulled up Zeus in front of a small building that had "Sheriff" painted over the door, but there were no lights on inside. He directed the horse to a large two-story building. It appeared to be the general store and the hotel. He tied Zeus to the rail out front and climbed down. There were two other horses tied to the rail. Samuel's hand slid down to his holster and loosened the hammer strap on his Colt, then gently lifted the rifle from the scabbard.

There was an old gentleman behind the desk tucked up under the staircase. He looked up as Samuel's boots echoed on the wood porch.

The first thing the man paid attention to was the star on Samuel's chest; then he took in the guns.

"Howdy, young man, what can we do for you? Need a room, or just some grub?"

"Sir, can you tell me if you have a sheriff?"

"Well, yes. In Crawfordville, about fourteen miles north of here. They keep an office here, but there's hardly ever a deputy there, unless of course we have trouble." The old man wasn't sure he wanted to know whether or not they were about to have trouble.

"Well, are you the only general store in Sopchoppy?"

"Yessiree! I'm the only old fool tryin' to make a livin' here." The old man grinned.

Samuel chuckled. "Well, then I guess you are the man I need to talk to."

The old man waited patiently while Samuel tugged a waxed pouch from his shirt pocket. He carefully extracted the flyer, now very creased. He turned it around to face the man.

"Have you ever seen this man before? He is a Choctaw Indian, possibly half white. He's a pretty big fella, about my size, only a little fuller around the chest. Goes by Nash, or Nashoba, for wolf."

The old man looked at the flyer. The moment he raised his eyes to Samuel's, Samuel felt a tightening in his stomach.

The old man began to speak. "Well, I don't rightly recall…"

Samuel slammed his large hand down on the countertop.

"Mister, I'm tired, I'm hungry, and I've been trailing a woman killer for almost forty-eight hours. If you are about to tell me a lie, I suggest you think it over really well. This man has kidnapped another woman and is headed west with her. Now, I know he trades in moonshine, 'cause he killed the one man in Tallahassee that he'd been selling to for years. I don't give a hoot if you've bought his liquor before, but if he comes through here again, he may be inclined to want to erase all his past dealin's with folks. Permanent like. Now, I'm gonna ask you again. Have you seen this man before?"

"Well, now that I look again…"

Samuel let out a long, exasperated breath. "Lately, like in the last two days?"

"No. No, sir, I haven't bought, I mean, I haven't seen him in over a year."

"So he has been here before, right?"

"Yes," said the old man, as he stepped back out of Samuel's possible reach.

Samuel shook his head. "I'm not gonna hurt you, sir. But I can't promise you that he won't. I'm hoping he'll make this his last "public" stop before he heads to Pensacola. He'll need some things, especially since he's got the woman with him."

Samuel's chest tightened just saying those words aloud. He'd been pushing forward, trying not to dwell on Kathleen or her possible condition. But speaking those words drove fear into his heart and mind. He couldn't remember the last time he was afraid. He'd given his own life and safety over to the Lord years ago. And he was just going to have to trust the Lord now.

"Sir, I could use a bed, just for a few hours. I'll be up long before daylight. And any warm thing from the kitchen will do me. Will you be here, minding the store all night?"

"Nah, we don't get much night traffic through here. The swamp to the west usually keeps most travelers from moving around at night. The train comes through at eleven thirty tonight, and then not again until tomorrow afternoon, around three. So I'll be closing the doors after the train rolls through." As he spoke, he took a key from one of the hooks on the wall behind him. He handed the key to Samuel.

"Number two, top of the stairs, to the right. Has a window that looks out on the street. You can take your horse around back, and the boy there will feed and water him. My old lady will run you up something hot in a few minutes."

"How much?" Samuel stuck his hand in his pocket.

"Oh, let's just say this one's on me. Seein' as how you warned me and all."

Samuel just looked at the old man. "All right, sir. But if he shows, and I'm not close by, don't let him get his hands on you. He's very strong. And very dangerous. You understand?"

****

Kathleen was so tired she couldn't sustain an intelligent idea, and her every muscle ached, but she was alive. At least for now. The sun had dropped below the tree line an hour ago. The temperature was falling, and the light was fading fast.

The man stopped his horse. He hopped down and walked back to her. He was still keeping her hands tied to the pommel, and her wrists were raw from the constant chafing of the rope.

"There is a village about three miles from here. We are going to pick up a few supplies. You will keep your head down and your mouth shut. Do you understand?"

Kathleen looked at the man in disbelief. If he believed she was going to just pass up a chance to tell someone she was being held against her will, he was the delirious one.

She raised her head defiantly, and then nodded yes.

The man let out an exasperated breath. He saw the tightening of her jaw before she nodded. Obviously she didn't understand. He would help her. He loosened her hands from the pommel, grabbed her by the waist, and jerked her off the horse. He held her with one hand while he open-handedly slapped her with the other.

It all happened so fast, Kathleen was not prepared. The first blow slammed her mouth shut, and she bit into her tongue. She could see the second blow coming, and could do nothing to stop it.

She was dazed, and her mind was running in slow motion. *This must be how Mary Elizabeth felt before she died. Oh, Samuel, I'm so sorry I didn't listen to you.*

Kathleen gathered all her strength and took a deep breath, preparing herself to fight back, when the voice filled her ear.

"No, dear, it's not the time to fight. You must think!"

Kathleen allowed her knees to buckle, and the man let go of her arms. She dropped to the ground like a sack of potatoes, curled up on her side, and lay still, expecting him to kick her.

The man knelt down, grabbed her arm, and jerked her to a seated position. He swiped her wild hair away from her face.

"Now do you understand me?"

Kathleen raised her eyes to meet his. There was no remorse in his eyes. *Think, the voice said to think.*

"I'm wearing a partially burned petticoat and only one shoe, there is a dirty bandage around my arm, and my face must look horrendous. Do you honestly think no one will notice?" She tried to keep the sarcasm out of her voice, as she spat out a mouthful of blood.

The man just knelt there, staring at her with blank eyes, as if she spoke a foreign language.

It was all she could do not to flinch when he stretched out a massive hand and pushed her hair away from her face again. And when he continued to stroke her hair, as if he were petting a dog, her stomach gave a mighty heave, and she vomited on his moccasins.

The man jumped up and took several steps back, as she pulled herself to a kneeling position and continued to heave. Finally, empty and weak, she rolled away and collapsed.

At this point, she didn't care if he killed her now.

She was surprised when the man shook her awake.

She was surprised that she had actually slept. It must have been the sleep of exhaustion. It was still dark, not the black of night but the gray of coming dawn. Her sleep-fogged brain tried to take in his words.

"Did you hear me?" he growled.

She tried to answer him, only to find her tongue so swollen it was difficult to speak. She must have taken a chunk out of it when he slapped her.

She tried again. "No, what did you say?" It was painful to speak, and to her ears it sounded as if she spoke around a dishcloth.

"I said, I am going to tie you to a tree before I go into town to get supplies."

She was awake now. He was leaving her here, alone in the woods, tied to a tree? What if he never returned? She would starve to death, or be eaten by something wild. She could feel the panic begin to rise. She didn't want to die here, alone. Her breath started to come in small gasps. She had raised her tied wrists to grab his arm, ready to beg him not to leave her, when she saw it.

Across the clearing was a woman. A tall woman, with long dark hair.

And then Kathleen heard the whisper. *All will be well. Let him go.*

She didn't think it strange that she was seeing the woman; after all, the woman had been whispering in her ear since the beginning of this nightmare.

She turned to the woman and said, "All right, but are you sure it will be okay?"

The man whirled around and looked behind him. There was nothing. He turned back to Kathleen and shook her.

"Who the hell are you talking to?"

Kathleen's confusion was clear, even to the man.

"Don't you see her, the woman with long black hair?"

"There is no woman," he shouted, as he shook her again. "NO woman, do you hear me?"

The message was clear: *Sshhh.*

She looked into his eyes and saw his fear. "That's right. Yes. No woman."

The man dragged her over to a small oak. He threw a blanket on the ground and set her on the blanket with her back against the tree. He untied her wrists but wound a rope several times around the tree and her middle before tying it off on the back side of the tree. He dropped a canteen down beside her.

"I'll be back." And he was gone.

Kathleen looked for the woman, but there was nothing but trees. She held her breath and listened intently, but the only sound echoing through the forest was the sad call of a lone owl.

Chapter Sixteen

The moon slid past the western horizon, and the darkness began easing toward dawn. Samuel had been awake for over an hour. He passed quietly down the staircase and made his way to the barn at the rear of the hotel.

"I see you're awake too," he said softly. "Sorry about the short rest, old buddy, but we've got to be ready when the time comes."

He finished saddling Zeus, gave him a handful of oats and a drink of water, and then walked him to the front rail of the store. He'd given some consideration to the best place to see both ends of town. While he didn't expect Nash to be taking a train, the roof of the station office gave a clear view of the east/west travel path, including the front of the store.

Since the train wouldn't be through again until this afternoon, Samuel didn't expect his presence on the roof to cause a stir. The office was closed up tight, so there was no one to see when he stood on the hand rail and swung his long frame up to the roof. He laid his rifle down beside him, checked the load in his pistol, loosened the strap on the knife in his boot, and finally settled down for the wait.

He thought about his decision to hover around Sopchoppy. He'd learned long ago to trust his first instinct. It was when you started doubting your own judgment that you made mistakes. The Lord had given him good instincts; he'd just had to learn to trust them.

****

The morning air was still chilly as Nash moved through the ground fog. Daybreak was held off a little longer by the cloudy sky. Nash was angry about having to leave the woman, but she was right. Someone would have noted her condition, and he couldn't very well kill everyone in town. No, it was best this way. He would pick up some pants for her in the general store. Then they would not have this problem again.

As he neared the edge of town, his wandering mind came to attention. He hated towns. He hated people, for that matter. They couldn't seem to mind their own business, always prying and asking questions.

As he rounded the bend coming into town, the fog lifted enough for Nash to see only one horse tied to the rail in front of the store. That was good. The fewer people to deal with, the better. He tied his horse to the rail and looked around. All was quiet in the still, chilly air. He lifted his rifle from the saddle, then stepped up the stairs and into the store.

****

Samuel had been so still that even if Nash had looked his way he wouldn't have been able to separate him from the brown rooftop. Samuel eased himself off the roof on the backside of the station and slowly made his way around the west end.

****

Nash found an old lady behind the counter.

"I need five pounds of cornmeal, five pounds of beans, and a pair of pants."

The old woman set her sewing on the counter and

looked up at the man. He was probably the biggest man she had ever seen.

"All right. The pants are on that table by the wall. You find what you want, and I'll get the staples."

Nash walked over to the table and held up a pair of denim pants. They were probably four inches too short for him, and nearly twice the width of the woman, but they would do, with a rope belt. He turned back toward the counter and detected movement through the large plate window. He believed he saw a man behind the station office, crouched over and moving quickly. He had not lived this long by ignoring his inner spirit, and it was screaming at him now. He made for the hallway leading to the back of the building. The old woman stepped out of the storeroom doorway on the left, blocking his path.

She gave a startled gasp. "You can't come back here."

Nash slapped her out of his way, and she crumpled to the floor, unconscious in a puddle of spilled cornmeal. Nash stepped out the back door and froze. He instantly recognized the old man, who was adjusting his belt as he exited the outhouse, about thirty yards away.

When the old man looked up, there was Nash, filling the doorway. The look on the Indian's face was enough to fill him with fear for himself and his wife.

The old man yelled, "What are you doing back here?" But he wasn't looking at Nash as he yelled.

In an instant, Nash knew the yelling was for someone else. So much for getting out quietly. Nash raised his rifle and shot at the old man as he ran around the east corner of the building.

Samuel was almost at the horse rail when the

shouting reached his ears. He bounded up the stairs into the store. A quick glance around told him the desk was empty, and he made for the back hallway. He was running so fast he had to hurdle over the old woman to keep from stepping on her. He heard the crack of a rifle as he ran. He slowed at the back door just long enough to curl himself into a ball, roll through the doorway and away from the building. As he rolled to his feet, he saw the old man on the ground. He'd raised himself up on one elbow, and when he saw Samuel, he pointed around the building to the main street.

Samuel paused at the front corner of the building, crouched, and peered around the corner. A shot flew over his head, and he jerked back. He lay flat on the ground and peered again. He saw Nash jump on his horse, grab for Zeus' reins, and head west. Samuel jumped up, gave a shrill, long whistle, and was rewarded with the sight of Zeus throwing his head down, locking his front legs, and turning toward Samuel while jumping straight into the air.

Nash was nearly unseated and had to let go of the reins. When he turned to get a look at the man chasing him, he saw a man who was almost his same size. A man whose face held no fear. A man wearing the star of justice on his chest. Nash turned back, kicked his horse, and headed west.

Samuel had a clear shot at his back, but could not take it. Where was Kathleen? Was she dead? He had to catch Nash.

Zeus was prancing when Samuel got to him. He slammed the rifle into the scabbard and vaulted into the saddle. Samuel could still see Nash in the distance. Nash's Tennessee Walker was strong, but Zeus was a

Florida-bred Cracker horse, and his stamina would outlast the Walker.

****

Kathleen was thirsty, but she was afraid to drink. What if this was all the water she would ever have? The sun was climbing higher in the sky, but the clouds were keeping the air cool. While she was grateful for this, she was fast losing hope.

She'd wiggled and twisted for a couple of hours, trying to loosen the ropes. All she had succeeded in doing was wearing herself out. If she could just go to sleep, then perhaps she would ease on out of this world while dreaming of Samuel.

"No, dear, that would not do at all. He would be heartbroken to find he had lost you. I know his heart, and he would never love again."

Kathleen raised her head slowly. She wasn't sure she wanted to converse with…whoever was keeping her awake. She slowly peered around the forest. There. There she was. Leaning against a tree. She appeared so serene. As if talking to a woman tied to a tree was an everyday occurrence.

"How do you know what's in Samuel's heart?"

"Because I was there when his heart first beat. And I saw the light in his golden eyes when he first recognized the mission the Lord had placed in that heart. And I felt the joy he felt when he realized you were his gift from the Lord."

Kathleen smiled weakly as she closed her eyes and leaned her head against the tree.

"Now, you must drink and you must rest, and all will be well."

Kathleen opened her eyes. She was alone. She

raised a hand to her forehead. Yes, she was hot again. Fever and the tightness in her chest would explain her state of mind. And of all things, she imagined she heard a hound baying.

****

Howard filled the canteen as he talked to Albert.

"Don't you ever let anyone tell you that you're not the finest tracker in the South. We're going on forty-eight hours, and you just want to keep on runnin'. But Albert, I gotta tell you, boy, I'm tired. I'm gonna need a couple hours' rest. Then you can drag me a few more miles. We haven't found any new sign since that piece of petticoat, but that girl must be smellin' high, 'cause you just won't give up."

Howard drew in on the twenty-foot leash until Albert was at his side. "That's right, boy, just lie down here with me for a couple of hours, and then we'll start again."

Albert looked at Howard with those big, sad eyes, lifted his nose in the air, and howled his displeasure at being interrupted on the hunt.

Howard rubbed the hound's back as he drifted off to sleep.

****

Samuel figured they'd been running for a couple of hours now. As long as he could keep Nash in sight, he was happy. The Indian had left the road a mile or so back, but that big ol' Tennessee Walker left some mighty-easy-to-follow tracks. They must be coming up on the Ochlockonee River basin, because the ground was getting wetter and softer.

They were running across a large field, toward what looked like the swamp, when the Walker screamed and went down. He caught up to the Walker just in time to see Nash wade into the swamp about fifty yards ahead. The poor horse had gone down hard and broken a leg. Samuel saw what looked like a couple of bones sticking out.

Samuel jumped off Zeus, drew his pistol, and shot the Walker. He tied Zeus to a cypress tree, then took off on foot. Nash probably knew his way around this swamp, but Samuel had never been in this area. He had to keep Nash in sight now.

Samuel had only gone a couple hundred feet before he was wet from his shoulders down. The mud sucked at his boots as he rushed forward, his pistol still in his hand. He took his eyes off Nash for a second to dodge around a tree and was suddenly slammed back into its bark by a white-hot burning in his right shoulder. His heart had been pounding so hard from the chase that it took a moment for his ears to recognize the sound of the gun.

"Damn," he muttered, as he ducked behind another cypress. He looked down at his shoulder. He could see the bloom of red spreading across his shirt. He flexed his arm, and the pain was bearable. Okay, he surmised, a flesh wound, no broken bone. As he edged away from the tree, he heard a scream.

He could now see Nash flailing in the waters ahead. He was fighting something. And as it took him down, Samuel saw the gator tail slice the air.

"*No!*" Samuel screamed as he pushed forward.

When he got within twenty feet, he could see the water churning red. Nash was keeping his head above water but was weakening fast.

Samuel drew his pistol and tried to get a bead on

the gator's head. Finally, he was able to get off three rounds. The thrashing slowly subsided, as if it took a while for the gator to realize he was dead. Samuel kept his pistol trained on Nash as he approached. When he was close enough to see the damage, he realized the gator had taken off a large chunk of Nash's left leg, high on the thigh, and the blood was leaving his body with every heartbeat.

Samuel holstered his gun and grabbed Nash under both arms as he looked around for some high ground. He had to drag the man about thirty yards before he could get him out of the water. There was no telling how many more gators were out there.

Once on solid ground, Samuel could see it wouldn't be long. The gator must have torn something serious.

"Where is she? Can you hear me? Is she alive?"

Nash could feel the blood rushing from his body, leaving him weak and cold. He could hear and see the man standing over him, but his mind was not processing. He'd seen men die from less, and he knew he was fading fast.

Samuel knelt beside him and grabbed him by the shirt.

"Answer me, damn you, is she alive?"

Ahh, Nash understood the man was looking for the red-haired woman. *My woman. My woman tied to a tree.*

Samuel could see it in Nash's eyes when the dying man understood his question.

With his last whooshing breath, he whispered, "Tree."

"Where?" Samuel shouted.

But there would be no answer.

Nash closed his eyes, as he could no longer see, but his ears picked up the single call of an owl.

Samuel leaned against a tree. His eyes filled with tears. He had failed. Kathleen was gone.

****

Howard was dreaming of a woman's soft whisper. No, she wasn't talking to him. She was talking to Albert.

"Yes, you've done a fine job of tracking, boy. You are almost there. Now wake your friend and get moving."

Howard was wakened by Albert baying like crazy and tugging on the leash Howard had tied to his belt loop.

"All right, all right, I'm awake."

Howard looked around him. Yes, he'd been dreaming. There was no one talking to anyone. He looked at the hound. Albert was wild eyed, running in circles, and baying nonstop.

"Okay, okay, let's go, boy."

Albert took off like a shot, as if he knew exactly where they were going.

****

Kathleen's body was racked by another coughing fit. Her chest was so tight that she could only draw short breaths. Pneumonia. It had to be pneumonia. She believed it must still be daylight; it had to be the sun that was causing her eyes to hurt. Her hands fluttered around the blanket she was sitting on, searching for the canteen. Finally finding it, she drank deeply. What did it matter if she drank it all? She was going to die anyway. They might never find her body. Lord, she was tired. Yes, she would just sleep her way to death. As her chin drooped and her conscious mind began to slip away, she could have sworn a wolf howled.

****

Howard cursed himself as he ran. He should have tied the darn rope to himself. He'd never seen Albert so crazy. It had caught him completely off guard. They'd been moving along at a good clip when all at once Albert just lunged forward, taking Howard to his knees. He'd scrambled to grab the rope, but Albert was gone.

Howard just kept following the sound of Albert's howl. Suddenly he noted the difference in the tone of the baying. Albert was giving that shorter, higher-pitched yelp. The one he used when he was getting near his game. Lord, had he found her? And was she alive? Howard jerked his pistol from the holster and ran faster.

He was close now. Albert was louder, but the baying intermittent. Howard fought his way through a half acre of thick underbrush, and when he plowed through to the other side, there they were.

Albert was running in circles around the tree, stopping every two or three passes to lick the woman's face. Even from this distance, Howard could see she was unconscious.

"All right, boy, calm down. We've got her now. You did a darn good job." Howard patted the hound on the head and rubbed his ears, all the while grabbing the rope and securing the animal to a nearby tree.

He dropped on his knees and cut the ropes holding Kathleen up. He could feel the heat coming from her body.

"Albert, it looks like we found her just in time. She's hot as blue blazes."

As he lowered Kathleen to the ground, he tried to get through to her.

"Ma'am, can you hear me? Ma'am, are you hurt anywhere?"

Howard looked around the small clearing. His heart jumped in his chest when he saw the horse tethered about thirty yards away.

So. She's too sick to make it back home. We've got to be close to Sopchoppy. I'll just get her on the horse and follow the railroad in.

Howard had always considered himself a reasonably good-sized man, until he tried to lift a six-foot-tall, unconscious woman up on the back of a horse. It wasn't pretty, but he finally got her up there, climbed up behind her to hold her on, and headed west, with a now quiet Albert trailing behind.

****

Under any other circumstances, Samuel would have made the effort to bury Nash, not that he deserved any dignity in death. But the wound in his shoulder was tightening up, the sun would be going down soon, and Samuel needed to make his way back to Zeus.

Samuel's mind worked independently of his body as he waded back through the dark water. There was no "if only I'd done this" or "if I had just been clearer about the gun."

Losing his mother at an early age had been the beginning of hard lessons learned. Life was a gift. A gift that was sometimes taken away too soon. Growing up early had toughened his emotions and strengthened what most folks called backbone, but none of that lessened the pain in his heart.

This was a pain like no other he'd ever experienced

before. All the "what could have beens" were filling his mind and choking off any rational thought. He heard a loud snort and realized he was standing beside Zeus, with no memory of how he had made it there. The horse was stomping the ground, not happy at having been left alone.

Samuel untied his old friend. As he climbed up in the saddle, his shoulder reminded him of his mortality. He was alive, and if he wanted to stay that way he had better get some help. He took the dishtowel he'd wrapped the biscuits in, two and a half days ago, folded it into a small square, and placed it inside his shirt over the wound to stanch the blood flow. He had no way of knowing the exit wound in his back was the real concern.

He patted Zeus on the head and said, "All right, boy, take me back to town."

****

Howard had never been so glad to see civilization, even if it was just a handful of buildings and a few people. His arms were about numb from holding Kathleen for what he figured must have been four miles. It was coming on dusk as he nudged the horse up to the rail in front of a two-story building. He sure hoped it was a hotel or boarding house.

"Hello!" he shouted. "Anyone inside?"

An old woman and a teenage boy peered around the door. The boy was holding a rifle out in front of him.

"Whoa there, partner. I'm Deputy Howard Wilkes, with the Leon County Sheriff's Office, and I have a sick woman here. I need some help getting her into a bed. How about puttin' that gun down and helpin' me?"

The old woman spoke up. "You can't be carryin' her all the way up those stairs. Just bring her to our quarters in the back."

Howard and the boy managed to get her onto a cot.

"I don't suppose you've got a doctor nearby?" he asked. He looked again at the old woman. She had a large bruise on the side of her face, and one eye was puffy.

The old woman shook her head. "No, but I sure could have used one this morning. First time I ever had to dig out a bullet."

Howard stood a little straighter. "You folks had some kinda trouble?"

"Well, that other deputy brung it with him."

"Where is he now? Ma'am, maybe you better start at the beginning and tell me everything you know."

She explained about the shooting as Howard listened patiently.

"Where is Deputy Hinton now?"

"Last anyone saw, he was chasin' that Indian out of town. Headed west, they was."

"And he hasn't come back?"

"No. And as mean as that Indian was, he ain't likely to. My poor Henry is only alive now 'cause the Indian was running when he fired at him. Just winged his arm. But the poor old soul's gonna need some rest. Too much excitement for us old folks."

"Well, I'm glad you folks are gonna be okay. When does the next eastbound train come through, ma'am? I've got to get that girl home."

"That'd be 'round eleven thirty tonight." The old woman looked at the clock on the wall. "You got about a five-hour wait ahead of you."

"Yes, ma'am. I wonder if you can get me some cool water. The poor girl in there is burning up with a fever. She had a coughing fit a while back, and I think she might have pneumonia. The Indian kidnapped her a couple of nights ago, and she's been through quite a lot."

"Well, lordy be, why didn't you say so?" She turned to the boy. "Freddy, run fetch a bucket of water, fresh from the spring. Now, run."

She turned to Howard. "I'll get my daughter, and we'll take care of the poor girl. You just have a seat and rest."

Howard was grateful to the woman. He hadn't been looking forward to talking to the schoolteacher, let alone trying to clean her up. Only the good Lord knew what she'd been through, judging by how the Indian had treated his past captives.

Howard didn't see Albert scramble up from under the table and take off for the front door. By the time he hit the front porch he was whining and baying. Howard's head jerked up at the sound, and he almost fell out of the chair he'd settled in. Good grief, he must have fallen asleep.

He was awake now. Albert was seeing to that. Howard quickly glanced around and finally found his rifle. He grabbed it up on his way to the front porch. He could see it was good and dark now, so he must have slept a couple of hours.

Howard put out the oil lamp by the door before he stepped out. No point in making himself a target. He eased out the door and put his back against the wall, straining to see what had upset Albert. He could finally make out a horse approaching slowly. As the horse got closer, he could make out the body of a man slumped over the horse's neck. When the horse stopped at the rail and whinnied, Howard realized it was Samuel Hinton slumped over the saddle, not the Indian.

Howard yelled, "Freddy," as he ran down the steps just in time to have Samuel slide off the horse and take him to the ground.

The boy ran down the stairs with a lantern but stopped abruptly at the sight before him.

"Well, don't just stand there, son. Help me roll him off, so we can see how bad he's hurt."

It took Howard, Freddy, and Freddy's mother, Alice, to get Samuel up the steps and onto a table in the kitchen. Once they tore his blood-soaked shirt off, they could see that the blood flow had stopped in the front of the shoulder but continued to seep slowly from the exit wound in the back.

Alice shook her head from side to side. "We're gonna have to stop that blood flow quick, while he's still got enough inside to keep him going."

While Howard rolled Samuel onto his left side, Alice took a jug off the shelf. She uncorked it and proceeded to pour it over Samuel's chest and back. He didn't so much as flinch as the moonshine washed his wounds. She then took a cleaver from a rack on the stove and held it in the oven's flame for a couple of minutes.

She turned to Howard and Freddy. "Ya'll better get a good grip, 'cause he ain't gonna like this." She waited until both of them were braced, then placed the cleaver against the exit wound.

Howard's insides churned at the sizzling sound it made, but he didn't have time to dwell on it because

Samuel screamed out loud and threw poor Freddy against the opposite wall as he reared up off the table. Howard held on for dear life, yelling the whole time.

"Samuel! Samuel, it's me, Howard. You're okay now, boy. Just lay back down."

Samuel was too weak to fight Howard. He fell back to the table. He was mumbling something. Howard leaned closer to hear.

"She's gone…gone…he won."

"Oh, no, boy, she's alive. I've got her right here." But it was too late. Samuel had lost consciousness again.

"Well." Howard sighed. "He'll find out soon enough."

****

When the train rolled in at eleven thirty, Howard Wilkes was ready.

He met the engineer and explained his problem. Every train had one man onboard who could run the telegraph if needed.

The operator opened the station office and telegraphed Tallahassee, and when the train pulled into Tallahassee, all was ready. It might have been two thirty in the morning, but the platform seemed filled.

Edward Finch was there with an ambulance and attendants. Garth Hinton was there to take the horses. Captain Lance was there to make sure his deputies were well cared for.

While Edward saw to the patients, Captain Lance met with Wilkes.

"So you're saying you don't know if the killer is dead or alive?"

"That's right, sir. The only time Samuel was

conscious was when we cauterized the wound, and that was only for a few seconds, so I haven't been able to ask him anything."

"Excuse me," Edward yelled across the platform. "I need to know Kathleen's history."

Howard Wilkes shook his head. "All I know, Doc, is that she was tied to a tree and burning up with fever when I found her. She had that big bruise on the side of her face already. She mumbled a few times as we rode to Sopchoppy, but it was never anything I could understand, but when she coughed I could feel her whole chest rattle." Wilkes could feel his face start to burn, as he actually heard his words.

Edward patted his shoulder. "Under the circumstances, I don't think she'll mind, Officer."

"But, Doc, there is one thing you should know. Samuel thinks she's dead. I wasn't able to tell him I'd found her. And you could tell he was real broke up about it. He just kept saying, 'She's gone.' "

"Thank you, Officer, I'll keep that in mind."

By the time Edward got the ambulance to the manor, Mae and Martha had set up a fine "hospital" room on the first floor. There was a dresser loaded with bandages, alcohol, and clean towels. They had hot water for the gunshot patient and ice in the icebox for the fever of either patient.

Edward took one look at Mae and put on his most stern "doctor" face.

"You, my dear, can just march right up those stairs and climb into bed. You will remember, please, that you are carrying what is probably twins, and you are almost seven months along. No, no, do not argue." Mae started pouring hot water into a basin to wash the blood off Samuel.

Edward was fully aware the bond between Mae and Samuel was far beyond the normal brother-and-sister relationship. He went to Mae and took her in his arms, and she rested her head on his chest.

"Mae, it is three in the morning, and if Samuel were to wake and see you standing over him, he would have my head on a platter for allowing you to put your health, not to mention the health of the babies, in jeopardy. You know this to be true. Now, I am going to have my hands full with these patients for the next few days, and I don't need the added strain of worrying about you. Do I make myself clear?"

He kissed the top of her head and turned her toward the door, where a waiting Martha escorted her upstairs.

The door had no sooner closed behind Martha and Mae than it opened again. Roxanne and Mrs. Peters marched in, bearing trays.

"Now, what have we here?" Edward asked. "Is there no end to the trail of women who insist on helping me care for Samuel?"

Both women raised their chins, but before they could speak, Edward laughed.

"Yes, I am fully aware that Samuel is a hero to every woman he has ever met. So...Mrs. Peters, pull up a chair for that tray, and start taking off that bandage on his back. Roxanne, help me get the clothes off Kathleen, and we'll see what we can do about this fever."

****

It had been a day and a half, and neither patient was responding as well as Edward would have preferred. Samuel had started running a low fever, which in itself was not bad, just proof that his body was trying to fight off any infection. But Edward was concerned over the loss of blood and the fact that Samuel had not wakened.

He had just sent Roxanne home to bathe and eat, and threatened that if she did not sleep for at least three hours he would bar her from the sickroom. The look she gave him as she left spoke volumes.

Edward checked Kathleen's temperature. They had gotten the fever to break about fourteen hours ago. The racking cough was aided by the mustard plaster Mrs. Peters had used three times now. Edward believed he might have time to slip into the kitchen and steal a cup of coffee, as both patients appeared to be in a peaceful, recuperative mode. He lowered the oil lamp and quietly left the room.

The flame in the lamp flickered, then sputtered out, leaving the room in a soft darkness.

Samuel was floating in a quiet place, a place which made no demands on his heart or his mind. There was something around the outer edges of his memory that he kept turning away from. Something painful and dark.

Samuel. Samuel, I know you can hear me. Listen closely, dear. It is time for me to leave you. You are no longer alone in this world. You have met your mate. She will be your strength, your inspiration, and your helpmeet from this day forward.

Samuel began to stir. Something was wrong. He needed to speak.

That's right, dear one. You must wake up now. She needs you as much as you need her.

Samuel's eyes blinked. He became aware of his

surroundings, and suddenly his mind translated what his heart had just heard.

"No! Don't go." Samuel thought he shouted, but in truth, his voice was barely a whisper. There was a cool touch on his forehead.

"Mama," he whispered, just as the door opened.

Edward almost dropped his cup of coffee. There she was. He'd only seen her for a few moments, six years ago, but this was something you never forgot.

And as the faint light around her began to fade, she looked straight into Edward's eyes.

"*I leave them all in your competent hands, my son. Goodbye.*"

And she was gone.

"No!" Samuel's voice now carried across the room.

Edward practically ran to his side. "Hey, brother, don't tear those stitches loose. Just lie back and let me re-light the lamp. Then I'll tell you a story."

Edward spent the next few minutes telling Samuel how he had arrived home.

"I'm really glad you have come back to the living. I was afraid I would have to tell Kathleen you didn't love her enough to live for her."

Samuel's confused expression was enough to let Edward know they had come to a critical moment.

"She's alive, Samuel. Wilkes found her while you were getting yourself shot. She has been very sick. And I'm hoping you can help me persuade her to wake up."

Samuel turned his head toward the other bed. His eyes filled with tears, so he closed them.

Edward cleared his throat. "Uh, Samuel. When I entered the room just now…" His voice trailed off.

Samuel opened his eyes. "She's gone. She said we

didn't need her now. That I didn't need her. That Kathleen would take it from here."

Edward slowly shook his head. "Then I guess that's that."

Chapter Seventeen

Edward had to drug Samuel to keep him from trying to get up and check on Kathleen himself.

"All right, brother, just let me get you something to drink first. You have lost a lot of blood and need to take in liquids." He said all this with his back to Samuel, as he stirred a goodly dose of morphine into the cup of coffee in his hand.

"Here, I'll hold it for you. That's it. Get as much as possible down. There you go. Now, hold still a minute, and just let me check that bandage before you try to get up."

Samuel lay back. Just the act of swallowing the coffee seemed to have drained him.

"Edward, how badly hurt was Kathleen? Does it look like…did he…hurt her?" Samuel closed his eyes. Edward grinned. As Samuel's breathing became shallow and rhythmic, he raised the sheet up to Samuel's chin.

"That's it, brother, sleep for now, and we'll take all the questions tomorrow."

****

When Samuel woke again, it was to see Sergeant Wilkes staring at him.

Samuel blinked his eyes several times. Howard was still there, so he must be alive.

"Howard, what are you doing?"

"Well, I was given orders to check on you. You and the schoolteacher."

Kathleen! Oh, Lord, how was she? Samuel jerked his head to the left, and all he saw was the wall. He turned back to the right, and there was a large curtain down the middle of the room.

"Where is she? She was here."

Edward spoke from behind the curtain. "Calm down, Samuel. I'll be right there."

The curtain parted enough to allow Edward to slide through.

"Now, what's all the fuss about? I have to tell you, Samuel, you are not a very cooperative patient." Edward stopped by the bed and took Samuel's wrist in his hand. "You seem to have slept well last night. Any pain this morning, other than when you flex your shoulder?"

"No, I'm fine. Where is Kathleen? Where did you take her?"

"She is right there, on the other side of the curtain. I figured I would not be able to keep you in bed after this morning, and that you might need a little privacy to wash up and change. But you're going to need to move slowly. I've kept you drugged for two days to give your shoulder time to begin mending."

The look Samuel gave him would have scared most men, but Edward was aware Samuel had good sense and understood that it was all done for the best, so he just stood there grinning like a boy who had played a prank on a friend.

"So, has Kathleen wakened yet?"

The grin left slowly. "No, not entirely."

"What does that mean?"

"Well, we've managed to get small amounts of broth down her, at various times. Like when she's mumbling. She keeps whispering she wants to sleep. That it's easier that way. Unlike you, she has not tried to leave the bed, so it was not necessary to drug her. So it concerns me that she continues to sleep. Now, as soon as your vision has cleared and you can keep down some broth, I'll let you bathe and see if you can talk to her."

Howard Wilkes cleared his throat.

Both Samuel and Edward had forgotten he was there. He had their attention now.

"I just have one important question to ask, Detective. Is Nash dead?"

"Yes, Howard, he is dead. We won't need to worry about him ever again."

Howard nodded. "Just one more thing. Did you kill him?" Howard had to make some kind of report, and while it didn't matter a hill of beans to him, one way or the other, the captain was going to want to know.

Samuel was slow to answer. His mind ran back over the pursuit.

"I would have killed him. I would have killed him in cold blood, if needed. But I didn't. He wrestled with a gator, and he lost. Gator took a large chunk out of his upper thigh, and by the time I could kill the gator, Nash was near gone. Every heartbeat was forcing out a stream of blood. I dragged him out of the water, and all he could say before he died was 'tree.' "

"Well, then we know that deep down somewhere he must have had some good left in him."

"What the hell gave you that idea?"

"He was trying to tell you she was by a tree. That's where Albert and I found her, tied to a tree."

Samuel slowly sat up and swung his legs over the edge of the bed. The room spun for a few seconds, so he kept his eyes closed. He finally opened them and looked at Howard.

"You're a good man, Howard, if you can give that killer credit for any human feelings. Regardless, it's done."

"Captain Lance said to tell you to take your time, get well, and then you can write your report." Howard grinned.

Samuel give his half smile. "Tell the good captain... Tell him I'll be in soon."

Samuel and Edward waited until the sickroom door closed behind Deputy Wilkes.

"Now, Edward, how bad is it that Kathleen is not waking?"

"Truth be told, Samuel, I'm not sure. She obviously has been through a deeply traumatic experience, being taken in the night, by a known murderer. She had a serious case of pneumonia, which Martha and Mrs. Peters handled without much help from me, I might add."

Samuel raised one eyebrow in question.

"Well, it seems that modern medicine has yet to find anything more effective than a mustard plaster, when it comes to problems with the lungs. And grateful I am for them—the ladies, I mean. And while the pneumonia was very hard on her, I believe Kathleen's refusal to wake up has more to do with her mental state than her physical one."

Samuel slowly stood, one hand on the bed in case the room started moving again. When it appeared he would be okay, he said, "I'd like that bath..."

He was interrupted when Martha bustled in. Patrick and Cyrus were right behind her with a large copper washtub. Their faces lit up with smiles when they saw Samuel standing on his own.

"Praise be!" Martha exclaimed as she dabbed at her eyes with the corner of her apron.

"Well, about time you got up and stopped lollygaggin'." Cyrus grinned. "I'd hug you, but you reek of swamp. So where do you want this tub?"

"Over here, boys, on this side of the curtain. You can fill it and then get out and let a man make himself presentable in peace."

Martha clucked at the foolishness. "I fetched you clean clothes and a towel, and…oh, here comes the water now."

Through the door marched a line of young women, each carrying a bucket of hot water to pour in the tub.

Edward stood shaking his head as they all marched back out, followed by Martha, Patrick, and Cyrus.

"It must be difficult, Samuel, being so important to so many people." Edward was grinning like a fool, as he headed for the door.

"I'd make you eat those words"—Samuel grinned weakly—"but I don't want my water to get cold."

"Well, just don't wet the bandage. I'll be back in a while to change it."

****

Samuel bathed as best he could with only one hand. He agreed with Cyrus: anything would be an improvement. He couldn't manage a shirt, so he just threw it over one shoulder. He opened the curtain in the middle of the room and positioned a chair beside Kathleen's bed.

The door opened slowly, and Mae peeked around the corner. Her eyes filled with tears the minute they found Samuel. She waddled across the room, her seven, almost eight months of pregnancy very much in evidence. Samuel stood and took her in his one good arm as she circled his waist with both hers. Samuel understood the feelings running through her.

It may have been six years past, but he would never forget the rage that had run through him when he saw Mae, battered and bloody from the attack made on her then.

She finally wiped her eyes and looked up at him. "It's a good thing you didn't go and get yourself really hurt, or I'd have been very angry with you."

Samuel softly kissed the top of her head and sat back down.

"Mae, how did you make it through your ordeal?"

It broke Mae's heart to hear the fear in Samuel's voice.

"Oh, brother, she'll work her way through all this. After all, she has you! Edward said he was sure, once she knew you were here with her, she would come out of this."

"But I was not there when she needed me most," Samuel whispered.

Mae replied, in her very best mother-tone, "Samuel Hinton, you don't get to decide when she might need you the most. That is up to Kathleen and the good Lord. You are here now, and that's what matters right this moment. Now, I'm going to have Cook send in some food for you. Edward told me I could have ten minutes only, and then I have to go back to bed. So you eat something, and after that you have one of the boys shove your bed over here next to Kathleen. Then you can just rest here all night and talk to her."

Good to her word, Patrick and Cyrus came in and arranged his bed next to Kathleen's. Martha visited with a tray of beef in broth, bread still warm from the oven, and pumpkin pie. She changed the bedding on Samuel's bed while she fussed over his lack of appetite.

"I'll just leave this tray, and you can eat whenever you get hungry. The doctor says he'll be in to check the little missy in a while."

Samuel gave her a weak smile in return as she quietly closed the door behind her.

He had eased into a light sleep when whispers reached his ears. He was immediately awake and extended a hand to touch Kathleen.

She appeared to be having a conversation with someone.

"But it hurts too much. I just want to drift away."

He cupped her face in his left hand. "Sweetheart, can you hear me? It's me, Samuel. Please, love, you must wake up."

She continued to plead with someone. *"But I don't want a life without him."*

Samuel was becoming alarmed. It sounded like she was resigning herself to death.

"Kathleen, wake up! Listen to me, not whoever is in your head. I need you here with me now. Wake up."

Samuel had not realized he was shouting until Edward burst into the room. "What the heck are you doing, Samuel? Why are you shouting?"

Samuel turned toward Edward, and Edward was shocked by the fear he saw in those golden eyes. In six years, he had never seen Samuel frightened, or even concerned, about anything except Mae.

"Do something, Edward! Make her wake up, please."

Edward was humbled that this extraordinary man, this hero to every female in the county, would be begging him to do something. He put his arm around Samuel's shoulder.

"Samuel, take a deep breath and let it out slowly. That's good. Now, it is not I you should be pleading with."

Edward could see that it took all of thirty seconds for the answer to come to him, and that delay was probably because of the drugs still in his system.

Samuel turned to the bed, sat in the chair, and took Kathleen's hand in his.

Edward could hear him praying as he slipped back out the door.

Epilogue

Samuel had prayed. And Kathleen had wakened.

Samuel stood at the French doors in the parlor as Charlotte ran circles around Kathleen. Kathleen sat in a chair, with her feet on a stool, covered by a quilt made by Mae and her mama years ago. A sunbonnet shaded her eyes as Charlotte danced and sang for her. Edward said it would take some time for Kathleen to regain her strength.

The county had called in a new teacher right away, and Kathleen had been here at the manor for a month now.

There was something Samuel needed to do, but he had waited until Kathleen had recovered enough to go with him. It would make for a long day, but Edward said as long as she didn't overdo physically, it would be all right. They would leave early in the morning.

****

"Yes, I know it's a surprise, but can't you at least tell me where the surprise is located?" It was useless to plead, but she enjoyed the teasing look on Samuel's face.

"You know what? The time would go by much faster if you lay down and took a nap, like I promised Edward I would make you do. Just lay your head on my thigh, and when you wake we will be there."

She was a little tired, which she would never admit

179

to Samuel, so she pouted.

"All right, if you won't tell me where we're going, I may as well go to sleep." She laid her head on his lap, pulled the quilt up to her chin, and drifted off to sleep.

As he drove, Samuel would occasionally glance down at that glorious hair and give a prayer of thanks that she was safe.

After today, Samuel could put all this behind him and start planning his future. One that included this wonderful woman and at least two or three children.

****

"Sweetheart, we're here. Wake up now." Samuel spoke softly, stroking her face.

Kathleen's eyelids fluttered as she stretched her long legs. When her feet hit the motorcar door, she remembered they had been driving. She sat up and looked around her. Good grief! They were in a cemetery.

She looked at Samuel, her confusion apparent in those green eyes.

"We drove all this way to visit a cemetery? And where are we, anyway?"

"We are in Trenton, where I used to live. My mother is buried here, and I need to speak with her."

Kathleen was a little taken aback, but she loved this man so much that nothing he did could be odd in her eyes.

Samuel lifted a blanket and a basket from the trunk of the motorcar. He held out a hand to Kathleen. "Come. It's not far, and there is someone I want you to meet."

It was a small, well-kept cemetery, with only a handful of graves. They moved to the far side. There beneath a towering magnolia was a single well-kept grave. The headstone read *Ruth Hinton, daughter of the Lord, adored wife, beloved mother.*

Kathleen's eyes filled with tears. What must it be like to be so beloved by your family, she wondered.

Samuel spread the blanket on the ground and took Kathleen's hand as she sat beside him.

"I wanted to talk to you about many things, Kathleen, and I believe this is the best place to do that. My life has changed a great deal since I met you." Samuel raised her hand to his lips, then smiled as he saw the blush bloom on her pale cheeks.

"Tell me about your mother, Samuel. What was she like?"

Samuel gave her his half-smile. "Be careful what you ask for, sweetheart. Seriously, that is why I brought you here today. To tell you how I feel, what I think, and what I want. And my mother is a great part of all that."

Kathleen smiled, leaned back against the tree, and made herself comfortable. "Well, I am your willing audience. Talk away."

"You know I was only eight years old when Mama passed on. For the next three or four years, Mae was the only female influence in my life. And then, one day, a strange thing happened. It didn't seem strange to me, but I wasn't sure how the rest of the world might feel, so I kept it to myself." Samuel stopped here, and turned to look Kathleen right in the eye. "My mama started speaking to me. Oh, not long conversations. Just occasionally she would tell me something I needed to know. Like the day she told me we needed to close the sawmill and go home 'cause Mae needed us."

The smile had left Kathleen's face, and her hand

had tightened its hold on Samuel's.

"Are you saying your mother actually spoke to you?"

"Yes. And the day Mae was almost killed, I saw Mama. There were others present, but they neither saw nor heard her. I talked with Pa about it later that day. I was sure he would think I was losing my mind. But he assured me that I was not. I see that you may have some thoughts on that matter yourself."

Kathleen had been looking down at the blanket. She immediately raised her eyes to meet his and gently touched his cheek, as she answered, "Oh, no, Samuel. You are one of the strongest, sanest persons I know, and I more than anyone..." Her voice trailed off as she stared across the cemetery grounds.

"What, Kathleen? Tell me what you're thinking."

"Samuel, we haven't yet talked about what happened between me and my sister's murderer. I know you have wanted to ask me questions. And I know that Dr. Finch probably told you to give me time. Well, it's time."

Kathleen raised her knees, wrapped her arms around them, and began talking.

"You already know that I did the one thing you told me not to do. I went out without the gun." Kathleen continued, telling him about the spider in the woodpile, which led to the broken lamp and the fire, and how Nash had actually saved her from being burned alive. She went on to speak of being afraid, of being sick from the spider bite and then from the cold rain.

"And then, well, I thought I was hallucinating. I kept hearing a voice. And each time I was about to do something dangerous, like try to fight, or yell, the voice would whisper in my ear. She kept me from making things worse, and she said, more than once, '*All will be well.*'" Kathleen was staring across the cemetery, caught up in her telling, and failed to notice how pale and still Samuel had become.

"And then, the morning he left me, I was so frightened of being left tied to a tree that I was going to beg him to take me with him, and she appeared. I could see her across the clearing. I turned to her and told her I didn't want to die there, and she said not to worry, that '*all will be well.*' Nash grabbed me and shook me, yelling that there was no woman there. So I just agreed. But I could see that he was very frightened."

She turned to Samuel and could see tears in his eyes.

"What did she look like, this woman that you saw?" he asked softly.

Kathleen considered a moment. "Well, she was almost as tall as me. She had very long, dark hair that hung loose, in waves." She paused a moment. "And...oh, dear Lord, she looked like an older version of Mae!"

She grabbed Samuel's hands. "Samuel, she told me that she was there when your heart first beat, and that she was there when you realized that...that you loved me."

Samuel slowly took Kathleen in his arms, and held her close to his chest. "Kathleen, I see you have already met my mother."

They sat quietly, in the shade of the magnolia, letting their minds absorb the moment.

Samuel was the first to speak. "She came and spoke with me, when Edward could not get me to waken. She told me you were alive, but that I would have to wake up and talk to you, because you thought I was dead and that you didn't want to live. She also told me that she was leaving me, finally, after all these years, because I had you now. That you would be taking over my care, from this moment on."

Samuel leaned away from Kathleen, and looked into her tear-filled eyes.

"I think you should know that Mama is never wrong about these things." With a grin, he continued, "I think you're going to have to marry me."

As Kathleen wiped tears from her eyes, she laughed. "It will be my greatest honor to marry you, and to hold your pure heart in my sacred care."

They held each other closely, as their minds looked ahead to the life they would share.

Somewhere in the distance came the call of an owl. Within seconds, there was an answering call.

If you enjoyed *A Man With a Pure Heart*, you'll want to watch for Linda Tillis's next book from The Wild Rose Press, Inc. Here's a sample:

A Heart for All Time

by

Linda Tillis

Chapter One

Asheville had some of the finest antique stores in the South, and Sarah was looking for something unique and affordable. She couldn't think of a better way to spend a three-week vacation.

"Oh, shoot," she said aloud, as she pulled the truck over to check her GPS. She must have written the address down wrong. She looked all around but could not find "Aunt Grace's Notions" anywhere. She was about to give up and go find some lunch, when she saw a small sign down an alley. She eased the truck down the narrow brick-lined lane, and there it was.

She was looking at a small building with green shutters. From the outside, it might have been any small, faded family business. But once Sarah stepped inside, she felt a shiver run across her shoulders. She knew she was going to find an exciting treasure here. The building was deceptively small from the outside. There were cases filled with glassware and old jewelry pieces. She could see the owner had set up little vignettes here and there: a beautiful chair accompanied by a Louis XIV side table; elsewhere a wingback chair with a matching brocade footstool.

Sarah must have been wandering around for at least twenty minutes when she heard a soft voice.

"Were you searching for something in particular, dear?"

She turned to find a slender woman standing behind her. Sarah had been startled by the voice, but now she stood speechless. The woman's head was covered in shiny, jet-black hair, except for an inch-wide streak of pure white that ran from the left temple back to a lovely chignon. Her prominent cheekbones and Romanesque nose spoke of Native American heritage, but her eyes were a deep, dark blue.

She smiled at Sarah and tried again. "Were you interested in furniture, jewelry, or maybe pottery?"

Sarah reddened as she realized she had been staring at the woman.

"I'm sorry. I didn't mean to stare, but you remind me of a beautiful old painting that belonged to my aunt."

The woman stood silent. After another embarrassing pause, she turned and started down an aisle.

"Come along, dear. I pride myself on helping people find just what their hearts desire."

As Sarah followed her, she realized why the woman looked so familiar. It wasn't just the hair; the woman wore a suede dress that hung loosely against her slim body. The neckline was covered in beautiful bead embroidery.

Sarah shook her head. She would have to look more closely at the painting in the den, but she was willing to swear this woman could have stepped right out of it. How odd.

The woman halted behind a glass case and observed Sarah, as if interested in her reaction.

Sarah looked down into the case and drew in her breath slowly. Her heart began to pick up its rhythm.

She was seeing some of the most breathtaking pieces of beaded jewelry she had ever come across in all her shopping trips. There were bracelets, brooches, and necklaces of all shapes and sizes.

One piece held her frozen to the spot. It was an upper-arm bangle. The shape, a winding snake, was common in a piece of this type. It was the jeweled look of the beads that called to Sarah. They were arranged in such a pattern as to perfectly resemble a diamondback rattlesnake with its head drawn back, as if ready to strike. The eyes were a golden-colored glass that seemed to speak to Sarah. She was so engrossed in study of the piece that she was startled when the woman spoke.

"She is lovely, isn't she?"

Sarah stuttered, "Excuse me?"

"The goddess. She is lovely."

"The goddess? Do you mean the snake?" Sarah raised her eyes to the woman. The woman was smiling indulgently, as if Sarah were a child drooling over a piece of candy.

"Would you like to try it on?"

Sarah watched eagerly as the woman opened the case and removed the bangle.

Sarah was not a thin girl. She carried twenty pounds more than her doctor was happy about. Years of working in the garden, carrying a rifle in the woods, and pushing first Aunt Thelma and then Uncle Frank in a wheelchair had developed some muscle in her upper arms. She felt a moment of insecurity as the woman extended the armlet. She would be embarrassed if it was too small.

It happened so quickly that Sarah was not sure

what she'd seen. It was almost as if the bangle had come alive and wrapped itself around her upper arm.

"It fits you perfectly."

When Sarah glanced at the woman, she thought she saw traces of a smug smile; as if she knew something Sarah did not. Sarah thought she must have imagined it.

"Yes," Sarah sighed, "it does fit nicely. And it's beautiful. But where in the world would I wear it?"

Sarah looked back in the case and saw a piece she had not noticed before. A beautiful arrowhead made of Tennessee Paint Rock Agate. It was suspended from a rope of aged rawhide.

"Now that, that would better suit my style."

She reached down to slowly remove the bangle from her arm. As she pulled on it, she felt a quick burn. She looked down at her arm. The bangle had come off easily and lay in her hand, but something on it must have caught on her arm, because she saw two little drops of blood where the bangle had been.

"Oh, dear," the woman exclaimed, "I am so sorry. You must have scratched yourself." She immediately produced a tissue and wiped away the droplets.

Sarah could barely see where they'd been. She handed the bangle back to the woman. "Could I see the arrowhead?"

"Of course." The woman placed the beautiful bangle back in the case carefully and then handed the rawhide rope to Sarah.

She held the smooth, cool, agate piece in the palm of her hand as she asked, "How much for this one?"

The woman smiled sweetly. "I'm not even sure where that piece came from. It is rather plain, don't you think? How about I just give it to you as an apology for the scratch?"

Sarah considered those dark blue eyes. "Are you sure?"

"Oh, yes, I am sure. Your heart says you must take this piece."

The woman's assertive tone made Sarah a little uncomfortable.

"All right, and thank you."

The woman started moving toward the front door. "Was there something else I can help you with?"

Sarah felt like she was being brushed off, but she didn't mind, as she suddenly felt tired. Must be all the overtime she had put in lately.

She followed the woman to the door. "No, ma'am, I think this will do me."

The woman smiled as she held the open door. "Yes, the heart knows what it wants."

Sarah heard the click of the lock behind her, as she headed for her truck.

****

She looked at the clock. Five-thirty. She'd taken a shower, thinking it would freshen her up, maybe wash away this tiredness. She was dressed in her newest jeans, matching jacket, and her favorite boots, with her revolver strapped above the boot top. The whole outfit went very well with her new arrowhead necklace. But now she wasn't sure she had enough energy to ride all the way into Greeneville for supper.

"Heck," she said to the empty kitchen, "I'm not even hungry now."

She opened the fridge, took out a full bottle of Sangria, and was reaching for a glass when she remembered the painting.

"Aha! That's what I was going to do."

Sarah moved to the back of the cabin, taking along the bottle and glass.

Both Thelma and Frank had been avid readers. He, of course, lived for the hunting magazines that came regularly, while Thelma had been a "closet" romance-reader. Uncle Frank had built a fireplace in the back wall of the cabin, and Aunt Thelma had arranged two reclining chairs in front of the beautiful river-rock wall, with an antique table between them to hold their bowls of ice cream. This had been their favorite retreat, the place where they spent hours reading, and dozing, completely comfortable in their love.

Sarah set the bottle and glass atop the table and turned to the inner wall. Yep, there it was. Aunt Thelma had once told her that the painting had been in the family for several generations. Sarah moved closer, to better see the details.

"Damn," she exclaimed. "I was right!"

There, before her eyes, was the woman from the store, with the same streak of white in her hair. In the portrain, she stood in a forest, with beams of golden light shining around her. Nearby was a large stag with his head thrown back, as if challenging her presence in his domain. She had one hand extended toward him as if to calm him.

"Good Lord," Sarah yelped aloud. There on the woman's extended arm was the snake bangle! Well, a snake bangle. Surely not the one from the store.

Moving to one of the recliners, she turned it to face the painting, then opened the bottle and poured a full glass of the cold, sweet wine. She got comfortable in the recliner and stared at the woman. She sipped occasionally, as she tried to make sense of it all.

****

Sarah was dreaming. Men were arguing. She was cold. She must have kicked the blanket off the bed. She reached out to feel for the blanket and felt dirt. The men were louder now. She must have left the television on. *All right, all right, I'll just have to get up and turn it off.*

Sarah opened her eyes and found herself looking at tree tops...and blue sky! She rolled to her side and found she was lying on the ground. Cold, hard ground. And those men were yelling and laughing on the other side of the bushes surrounding her.

Sarah froze. What the heck was going on? She slowly reached down and removed the revolver from her ankle holster. She heard a man yelling, and what he said made her blood run cold.

"Taggart, you'll never get away with killing me. You'll be the first suspect when I come up missing."

"Hell, Kramer, they'll think you finally went off the deep end and hung yourself. If they ever find your body. I mean, we are a far piece up the mountain, and why would they come looking up here?"

"Folks'll just say the poor soul couldn't get over his wife and kid dying while he was off roundin' up horses. Got the best of him, livin' in that house...lookin' at all those pictures he drew."

Sarah heard several voices laugh.

"And after a few months, I'll just go into town and lay a claim on the place, pay any back taxes, and it'll all be mine."

Sarah crawled closer to the bushes. She could just make out a man on a horse. His back was to her, but she could clearly see the rope around his neck. Oh, Lord, she had no idea how many men were there. Her gun only held five rounds. Without even realizing it, she started to pray.

"Please, Lord, help me. Please don't let them hang this man, Lord."

A word about the author...

Linda was born in Goody, Kentucky, in the heart of coal mining country. Her mother moved her to Cleveland, Ohio, when she was a small child. In the summer she ran barefoot on her grandparents' farm and during the school year she attended concerts and visited museums. She was able to experience the best of both worlds, city and country.

Her careers have been just as varied. She spent eighteen years in the manufacturing end of the fashion industry, which fed her love of color and style. From there she went on to spend twenty years as a Crime Scene Investigator. This gave her an insider's perspective on the abuse of women and children.

You will find her stories are of strong women who have overcome adversity to find the love and stability they deserve, and there will usually be a milliner involved.

http://lindatillisauthor.com

Thank you for purchasing
this publication of The Wild Rose Press, Inc.

If you enjoyed the story, we would appreciate your
letting others know by leaving a review.

For other wonderful stories,
please visit our on-line bookstore at
www.thewildrosepress.com.

For questions or more information
contact us at
info@thewildrosepress.com.

The Wild Rose Press, Inc.
www.thewildrosepress.com

Stay current with The Wild Rose Press, Inc.

Like us on Facebook

https://www.facebook.com/TheWildRosePress

And Follow us on Twitter
https://twitter.com/WildRosePress